Fauun

Born in Brisbane in 1972 and raised in the freshly carved
suburbs of Australia's Logan City, Fauun grew into a
storyteller of all mediums. After a three-decade career
as a designer, director and creative director — living
and working in Sydney, Montreal and Paris, Fauun
returned to Australia inspired, and committed to
writing full-time. Fauun's leap of faith cascaded into
a series of significant life events. The years to follow
saw her endure the seasons of divorce, financial ruin
and homelessness, which resulted in living in her car
while a student of her new path. Fauun's first novel,
1991, is inspired by her own personal story as a young
artist caught in a violent relationship, in the wake of
her lifelong friend's sudden death. Fauun currently lives
on the Gold Coast, Australia.

1991

by FAUUN

Fauun—1991

First published in Australia 2020 by Fauun.
First Edition. © 2020 Fauun

The moral right of Fauun to be identified as the author
of this work has been asserted.

This is a work of fiction. Any resemblance to actual persons,
living or dead is entirely coincidental.

Published by: Fauun, PO Box 301, Burleigh Heads,
Queensland 4220 Australia

ISBN-13: 978-0-646-82760-5 (Hardcover)

ISBN-13: 978-0-646-82749-0 (Digital)

ISBN-13: 978-0-646-82663-9 (Paperback)

A catalogue record for this
work is available from the
National Library of Australia

Cover design by Fauun.
Typeset in Cormorant Garamond.

www.fauun.com

*Fauun acknowledges and pays respect to the Yugambeh people of the
Gold Coast and all their descendants both past and present. We also
acknowledge the many Aboriginal people from other regions as well as
Torres Strait and South Sea Islander people who now live in the local
area and have made an important contribution to the community.*

for Mark
(1971-1991)

CONTENTS

Some things in life don't seem to have a beginning or an ending. You can't be sure if these things nourish or erode your soul—but you still let them consume you as if entranced by a flame, waiting to be burned.

CHAPTER ONE

Edie, Caio Baby

Ash was early for her one o'clock appointment, tired and ruined, like a forgotten teenage beauty queen. Her hair, decadently long and blonde with blanched strands of pink, once a shock of colour, had succumb to the grief. Her eyes, so heavy and blue like a vintage doll, you would expect her to blink when tipped back and forth. Her tiny body was propped upright by perfectly athletic legs punctuated with scars. She carried a gaudy orange fur coat on her neatly folded arm, like a jockey at a weigh-in. Edie found that coat for Ash while rummaging through a Paddington thrift store, so long ago. When she was still alive. Before all of this. When orange was unobtrusive.

The clinic waiting room was a shade of green never before imagined, and hopefully soon forgotten. The walls cast a colour that exuded doom for the ill to bask in. The fluorescent hover of light only gave way to the darkened corners, where the room's extremities quietly flaked and peeled. Ash expected the walls were ageing in the most secret places deliberately, as an act of awful self-preservation. In recent weeks, Ash had made a correlation between colour and truth. As the colour drained from her world, devastation set in.

Dr Leloyd was a strikingly bland character. Ash had observed during the last three visits that his complexion, mixed with his outfit selections, made him appear like a beige smudge. The drone of his voice lived up to the expectations of the stale room. Words hit flatly against those green walls and slipped from Ash's memory. She was now fixed on the clock that was suspended like a halo above the Doctor. At just seven minutes past one, Ash marvelled at the creep of time. It made her so tired. She was exhausted by the idea that there was another seven minutes ahead. She searched the room, bleary eyed, for something to look at, somewhere comfortable to rest her gaze. The high narrow window brought no solace as it framed the dark clouds that marched toward the Highlands from the sea. So for now, the crazed orange cuffs of her coat would do. There was nothing sympathetic about orange and only seemed to stare back at Ash with overbearing intent.

Dr Leloyd, was an old friend of her Father, Henry Smith. They met in the university cafeteria during an exam break when Henry fainted after realising he had a nosebleed. Henry had always been like a canary in a coal mine. This was consistently reflected in his reaction to life itself. *'Living is not for the faint-hearted,'* Henry would say, amusing himself with the impression he was both humorous and philosophical. Unfortunately, being faint-hearted, meant he had neither of those fatherly attributes, and was known to faint often.

The Doctor pushed back into his chair and made his closing statement. He spoke in riddles for a long while, then sat forward, without the bother of standing up, to indicate the session was over. Ash's face was invaded by a weak smile, made compulsory through the unseen forces of politeness. Otherwise void of emotion, she agreed with the Doctor, closing her eyes and pausing with a slow inhalation before breathing out her words.

'Yes Doctor, I will. It is time... a new path,' she hoarsely recited.

Dr Leloyd removed his outrageously ugly glasses and suddenly rubbed his eyes as if a blast of sand had hit him. Ash was afraid the Doctor would imminently show some emotion, which gave her an urgency to leave. She felt the weight of standing with a heavy heart and steadied herself by focussing on her ravaged Chuck Taylor All-Stars. One step at a time, the exit would eventually arrive.

The first gulp of crisp air tasted like serenity. Ash breathed in the wild bird song, and in return, chose not to cry. Sidestepping faster than she would like down the wet driveway of the hospital, Ash wished she'd brought her skateboard to gently roll her away. Roll her home, if that's even where she wanted to be. Ash recalled an old Joni Mitchell song while sliding incrementally in the drizzle, something about skating all the way home. With a feeling of relief, she neared the sanctuary of the curb.

The brisk afternoon chilled her hands, and she fumbled to locate her rattling orange pockets that were swinging freely at her sides. Ash was weaponised with little pills for the grief. She won't be needing them. Edie never liked pharmaceuticals. Now a sole surviving twin, Ash realised that she may have to compensate for them both from now on. *No pills.* She chose organic pain, for Edie, and made room for it. She wished she could say the same for their Mother, Joan Smith.

The birds cried sourly in winters' cage. Their pitch dared to penetrate the walls of Mrs Smith's formal lounge room which was committed to silence on the first Monday of July, 1991. The last day, here on earth, for Edie Smith. Daylight narrowly overstepped the boundary of the heavy floral drapes, interrupting the dim cloud of grief that had been carefully maintained by her Mother ever since. The lounge room sat vacant, except for the relentless wall clock. Persistent, like the birds. Nobody complained.

Lined with richly flocked wallpaper and deeply coloured décor, the room set the stage for the tightly upholstered velvet couch. Golden and virgin, it was normally reserved for parental intervention of the Smith twins. Overhead, and perhaps disproportionate to the room, hung a freshly framed photo of Edie in living colour. Beside it, a delicate crucifix, anguished and insignificant.

A much smaller photo of Edie with her identical twin sister, Ash Smith, sat on the walnut side table, beside the telephone. Its receiver was off the hook, as it usually was of late, to maintain a sense of dark solitude. An arrangement of long-dead white roses with a *Sympathy* card embedded, sat to the side amongst a puddle of exhausted petals. The clock struck two. The hour reverberated in the room without witness.

Despite the careful perfection of this room, the door creaked as Mrs Smith entered. Her high heeled footsteps followed rhythmically, and almost regretfully, as the mourning woman wished for silence. She crossed the room and picked up the receiver to put it correctly on the phone. With the softest click, the Smith residence was reconnected and equipped for outpourings and the social logistics of bereavement.

The Smith residence was the neatest on Bowery Street. The single storey house was small yet grand, if that was even possible. The sandstone bricks, so old and weary, they were pitted with holes, like crazed ants had made a meal of them over a hundred years. The timber adornments glossy and fresh, couldn't be smoother and so perfectly straight it made no sense. The partial renovation was an attempt by Mr Smith, an architect, to bring some balance into the presentation of his suburban abode. An attempt to control his environment had helped him make amends over the years. Amends with himself. Since given an option for early retirement back in 1987, Henry had taken to horticulture. He was quick to find the science behind it full of inexhaustible possibilities. Henry didn't need to hear that it was also an art form. The science was enough to engage him full time, however, the outcome was an everlasting work of art infused with secret memories of his girls.

The smell of green ants stung the air as Ash realised Edie would never wander that lawn again. She left footprints on the dewy underlay of the blue couch turf as she dragged toward the stone path. The Japanese camelia took a delicate form, with a dense habit and a bloom that would pierce the morning fog with a pink so full of intent, it would make the fuchsias blush. The rose of winter would stop Edie in her tracks on those cold days, as she climbed the mossy stairs, she inhaled the garden while heavy with books. Her literature about literature. Nothing but love stories.

Henry couldn't have found more joy in designing and building his own glass house. Once erected, he was able to harness nature and control the environment of his plants, way beyond the limitations of the Highland's seasons. His favourite plant, at the time of construction, was the *strelitzia*. In hindsight, Ash found this ironic. This flowering plant needed warmth, lots of it, and light, and it literally stole the attention from anything else nearby—nothing like Henry. Ash imagined the bird of paradise, the most ostentatious flower of them all, would be almost offensive toward the other species in the garden. Orange, purple, pink, tall with a beauty defiantly out of place. The Henry Smith Strelitzia was quite possibly the only one of its kind for a thousand miles. Edie too, loved this flower above all others. But her attraction to it made perfect sense, in hindsight.

The front doorstep was immaculate. The doormat rested in precise alignment to the threshold. *Welcome* was definitely not ready for Ash's damp Converse. *Not welcome.* It dawned on Ash that it was time to leave, not come home. Those mossy steps were not going to provide a new path. The path to this house was the antithesis of where Ash needed to be.

Joan Smith was sitting at the kitchen table. Ash was surprised to see her out of bed. The dreadful daylight fell all around. Mrs Smith pressed her palms flatly on the antique cypress. Ash wondered if her Mother was admiring the fact that there was not a single speck of dust breaking its sheen. Edie's wrists were slapped more than once as a teenager, for pointing out to her Mother that cypress wood was for coffins, not kitchen tables. Edie said it was bad luck, and this turned Joan's mood black. Edie knew all about trees, like an old Druid.

Such details seemed so important in the past. Year on year, the sterility of their home had caused calamity and catastrophe. In a child's eyes, this was how a mess could be measured. It was to be expected that for the remaining Smiths, there was no measure of the mess that had occurred since the first Monday of July.

'Mama?'

'Ash. Please, I just can't.'

'Look at me?'

'It's too much, I need a break.'

'Are you going away?'

'No, I can't. Who will look after your Father?'

'Dr. Leloyd said I should find a new path. Make a fresh start.'

'It's hard to see Edie at every turn in this house.'

A stifling reality had finally become malleable. Ash felt pushed out of the nest. One baby died, the other left to fend for herself as the Mother abandoned the nest, and the Father? Well, he didn't interact either way, bless him.

The hallway was the darkest place in the house. As a corridor of closed doors, it also seemed the longest path for Ash to take. From the kitchen to her bedroom, somehow passing Edie's bedroom door without her heart stopping, seemed an insurmountable distance. Edie's bedroom was like an alchemist's cave laden with other worldly treasures. Edie was always at ease with the occult, and was well aware of the forces of nature. She found it endlessly fascinating that these powers could be harnessed—should one be so inclined. The large bay window that illuminated Edie's room encroached on a garden bed of foxglove with beautiful clusters of purple flowers that seemed to levitate in the low light. Any curious creature would soon succumb to the little purple bells, should they stop for a taste. This always worried Edie and she often asked Henry to remove the deadly plants. Henry never got around to it.

Ash's bedroom was at the end of the hall. It was certain that when she would leave home, she'd miss the unashamedly delightful shade of lemon painted on the walls and the way the garden shadows gently stroked her bed in the afternoon. Ash filled her backpack. She'd often wondered what kind of things she would grab if the house was on fire. Edie's dog-eared Seawitch tarot cards, Polaroids, sketchbook and her best pens, incase she wanted to write something good. Skateboard. Yes. And bikinis, since this was not a drill. Ash decided not to be cold anymore. Doctor's orders.

The late sun darkened as Ash tread lightly on the sodden path that meandered through the burial plots. An enormous Himalayan oak tree was central to the cemetery, rising like a spike to the heavens. With a rush of cold air announcing dusk, Ash wondered if its roots entwined warmly with the dearly departed. She meditated for a moment, wondering what lay unseen beneath her, underground. Down, down, down. Edie once told Ash that oak trees were cosmic storehouses of wisdom. Was the wisdom above or below? Cosmic wisdom. Did it hover like fireflies in the ether? Was it inside all of us, dormant until we communed with the oak as Edie had? She always found it easy to float between two worlds. Edie had a hypnotising beauty and an ancient mind. She was ethereal; that was her witchcraft.

The cemetery had many new graves. That first Monday of July, the most greedy day of all, took more than Black Ridge could ever afford. Ash's heart squeezed with guilt when she couldn't immediately recognise Edie's plot amongst the other new additions. She continued to amble, heart racing, mind galloping, and tears burning in her head. Under a mass of plastic wrapping and contorted brown roses, there was Edie. Far, far away, now curled in the embrace of the old oak tree. Ash felt weakened by the sight and felt compelled to lay on the grave. A moment of surrender on this bed of thorns. Still in her oversized orange coat, her backpack tipped awkwardly, and her skateboard lay belly-up on the grass—so bright but lifeless.

The sun fell away, finally letting the environment grow as colourless as it yearned to be. In time, Ash rose. She released her grip of the freshly cut *Henry Smith Bird of Paradise* and tentatively placed it on Edie's headstone. First she whispered, then she howled.

On the highway, the sprawling horizon was pressed heavily under the cold purple haze. The sun had fallen behind the mountains and darkness would soon cover the path. The bus lowered itself, silver and glistening, as it inhaled the last light of day. Set heavy on the black ribbon that was pulling the vehicle north, Ash pushed back into her seat, tipping her face to the skylight, encouraging gravity to stop a tear which was poised to fall. The interior atmosphere of the bus, warm and transformational, promised her the immense silence she needed. The windows now only offered an internal reflection, framing a girl who refused to admit she was lost. The coach pushed into the night as if time and distance were one of the same, and of no consequence.

With just her skateboard and backpack, Ash had flown the coop. Blindly and wildly, with a baseless trust that by forcing the hand of destiny would bring reward.

Dawn burst like a cloud of sawdust across the plains. The last few hours of the journey pulled Ash's attention toward the rolling landscape. Dry earth dusted with wheat coloured vegetation, parched and bowing to the roaring highway. Farmhouses huddled in corners to make way for acres of sugar cane and the rusted iron monsters that harvested it. Then, the most lush rainforest carved by tired rivers of bitumen with stoney, frayed edges.

As the bus heaved over a peak, the shimmering coastline was revealed. The coach felt like it had to walk down the mountainside, but the passengers didn't mind as they feasted on the horizon, drinking in the possibilities of the new day. A road sign peppered with bullet holes, leaned into the undergrowth, *Gold Coast 40kms*.

CHAPTER TWO

Pretty In Pink

A landscape of girls evaporated the sun. They watched
the pack of surfers walk towards the shoreline in the
blinding light. These boys were different from the
others. Outsiders. Long matted hair and not quite well-
done tattoos. Their posture arched like hungry wolves
as they scanned the heaving waves. Their sharp jawlines
cut through the air ahead of them as they closed in on
their lover, the sea. With wetsuits half on, like shed skin
dangling from their hips, they had narrowed their focus
and chosen their prey. Impossibly tanned and lean, the
five young men reached the frothing edge as she beckoned them in. The water retracted, leaving the sand
gasping and pockets of air escaped in small explosions
around the surfers' feet. The wolves put their surfboards
ever so gently on the white sand. They adjusted their
armour without a sound and engaged. Out they paddled
fiercely, like a flock of gulls closing in on a decanted
fish, before escaping out of view under the pounding
waves. The sea, now wanting to overthrow them, pushed

back with every breath, before drawing them inside her. From the shore, it looked like a fight. From the water, it looked like love, as the surfers immersed their bodies forcefully into her curling embrace.

One of the surfers broke away from the clutch. Jay was searching for more. There were days when the sea was not enough. She didn't throw him the challenges he craved. He liked it when she hit back forcefully in unmeasured response to the rage he expected her to dissolve. With a clenched jaw and fierce paddle, his spirit inviolable, trapped in the confines of his body. Today he felt explosive. Invincible. His long hair, golden and pale, clung to his broad shoulders and snaked down his wet back. For nineteen, Jay looked formidable. Eyes, blue and steady. A heart-shaped mouth softened the blow of his triangular face, which reinforced his intimidating posture. On the inside, in contrast, one could see something softer and broken like a mistreated kaleidoscope. Jay had been gifted the intelligence to disguise all of these extremities, enticing the most delicate flower without her noticing she had lost her petals.

In a bikini the colour of pink lemonade, with her hair trailing behind like a velvet rope, Ash was a blaze of beauty as she projected herself along First Ave. Her tanned bare feet, dusted with glittering sand, she expertly guided the skateboard up the street. She embodied a natural grace that made all the local girls cry. Ash approached the pack of male surfers, looking like wet dogs limping home to feed. The five strangers walked along the road forming a human blockade.

They had a code that Ash was not party to. The new girl. She rode through the group of men, breaking the line. Ash otherwise went unnoticed by the pack who were caught in the verbal dissection of their surf, except for one of them. Jay had *seen* her. His pounding heart broke his rage into particles of light. Then she was gone.

Arriving at the little servo on the corner of Monaco Street and the highway, Ash fought her way into the phone booth that had a broken door. It barely seemed made to human scale. Clutching the truck of her skateboard and a shred of newspaper, she was pressed against the scratched glass. She picked up the receiver and dropped a coin in. After hesitation, Ash dialed a number known by heart. She waited patiently for an answer, cupping the receiver between her ear and sunbaked shoulder, her eyes unconsciously cast to the ground.

The dull tone persisted, and the phone remained unanswered for the longest time. Disappointed, Ash hung up. She took the refunded coin from the telephone and considered calling home again, finally choosing not to. It had been a month since she left Black Ridge. A month since she tried to look into her Mother's vacant eyes. *I'll call again tomorrow,* she thought. Ash wiped her cloudy stare and looked at the inky piece of newspaper she was thumbing. Her stomach churned as she realised she had slowly been eating through her list of last resort ideas to make ends meet away from home. To her own disdain, she had turned to her most obvious asset, her body. Nervously, she found her composure, and lifted the bulky old phone receiver one more time. She adjusted her posture and carefully dialed the number on the tiny classified clipping. Surprisingly it rang only once, a Scouse accent answered, barely interested enough to speak.

'Yep?'

'Hello...umm. I'm calling about your ad in today's paper, swimwear models wanted. No experience necessary.'

'Yep.'

'I'd like to apply.'

'Oh right, the glamour model ad. Do you know Sixty Six Studios?'

'No. I've—'

'Sixty-six, the Esplanade, Surfers. Clean hair, no make-up. Four o'clock.'

Click.

Ash caught her reflection on a mirrored panel in the phone booth and stared blankly at her distorted face. She put the receiver down too slowly, collected her thoughts and her skateboard before she rode back to Zoe's place to prepare for the photoshoot.

Four o'clock arrived too soon. Dan was looming over Ash with his camera as she reclined on a shag pile rug, thick and white like a symmetrical cloud on the studio floor. The white string bikini was dangerously small. The Lycra bows rested on her curved hips as she rocked from side to side, searching for the elusive angle of her body that the photographer was insisting on.

She arched her back, her young breasts needing no encouragement to command attention under the thin smear of the translucent bikini top. Her eye make-up was black and heavy like molasses, only making her blue doll eyes shine in a way that made her feel ashamed. Her mouth was red and glossy, like a bowl of cherries. Her cascade of hair fell like long fingers into the soft rug as she tipped her face to the light overhead. Ash had the body of a thoroughbred, mismatched with the innocence of a fawn. She didn't know her power in a superficial world and continued to cower under the ravenous gaze of man. Through all of this, Dan finally concluded that Ash was too tense. In response, she awkwardly changed position under his impatient voice. She swung her hair and lifted one knee for a moment, flexing her left flank and causing the photographic assistant to look elsewhere. He quickly re-focussed his attention on the reflector. The photographer glowered.

'Chin down... good. Eyes to me luv. Head to the left. No. Arch your back. More, more, more.'
'How about I change my pose?'
'How about you sit up luv. We're just warming up.'

Ash smiled apologetically and changed her approach, knowing full well she was losing her poise. She started adjusting her bikini top, looking for some-where to hide inside the pair of tiny triangles.

'Now there's a good idea. Yes, take your bikini top off luv. Not all the way, just undo it and hold it so we can see it's falling off.'

The photographer moved in closer to entice Ash. He reached out to adjust her hair with his sausage like fingers causing Ash to instinctively recoil.

'Trust me... I can get you into a magazine you know.'
'No...'
'Ok. I think we're done. I don't have time for this. Get dressed and get out darlin.'

Frustrated, the photographer popped open the camera back and yanked out the film, destroying the exposures. He waddled away, belly forward, shoulders back. To add extra drama, he tossed the spent film into the rubbish. It landed with a satisfying clang.

'Bloody useless!'

Stunned, Ash stood like a gazelle spreading her wings, hardly able to balance as she comically teetered in the oversized high heels.

'Shame you couldn't deliver, not the best *try out* I've 'ad this week. The other girls had no trouble showing a bit' a skin. They could see the potential. They understand art,' he whined.

Behind the dressing screen, Ash fought back anger and tears. She fought to take off the bikini top, which was knotted behind. With her frustration escalating, her hair tangled with the top and after considerable struggle, she eventually freed herself. Thinking she could have the final furious word, she scrunched the bikini top and threw into the studio space. It landed silently, of course. Her rage was cute.

Once dressed in her clothes, she humbly stepped away from behind the screen and looked helplessly at the dishevelled photographer.

'Sorry darlin. No pics, no pay.'
'No wait, I need the money. Please, I'm... I'm sorry.'

Ash picked up the thrown bikini and meekly handed it to him. He snatched it like a spoilt child.

'Not my problem. You gotta lot to learn angel.'

Ash backed out the door onto the pavement. The sun was low and the palm tree shadows were creeping. Ash wanted to let go and just break down. She wiped her eyes and started walking. As she paced she fixed her hair, removing the pigtails and ignoring a couple of guys who were taking a long look at her. She wiped the lipstick from her cherry mouth. Her panda eyes were growing darker as she strode forward. She wished she could vanish like Edie.

Ash stepped onto a Surfside bus, walked down the back and sat exactly in the middle. The sunlight pushed in and filled the empty seats. Meditatively, she enjoyed the warm light on her smudged face. She gazed out the window, watching lines of palms and lamp posts rhythmically pass by.

'Beach Road. Beach Road!' the driver called.

Then the bus jerked to a halt. Ash clamoured toward the exit.

CHAPTER THREE

Paradise City

Everybody knew 1991 Monaco Street was more than a house. It was a breeding ground for mayhem. It was magnetic. It was a wolves den. It was where the pack feasted on their night's catch. Where lost boys would seek shelter. Nobody could resist the lure of this dilapidated quinta and the legends of languid misfortune that hovered. Gossip about the boys that lived in this house spread along the boardwalk from Main Beach to Nobby's like a virus. It was poetic to compile the facts and the fiction. The tales of misadventure seemed to bleed from the house, and the consequences vibrated in the silent walls. The reality, of course, was always less fantastic, but notable when recalled.

There were always whispers—*They sold weed. They surfed. They skated. They hitch hiked. They woke up lost, had mongrel dogs, smashed cars, wandered. They surfed every dawn. They surfed at night, pulled bongs for breakfast, robbed stores, stole cars. They knew the pushers, the strippers, the* club owners, the freaks, the thieves, millionaires, models, the police, pro surfers, shapers, rockstars and the nobodies. They were watched. They were chased. They smashed stuff. They burned stuff. They dumped stuff, carried knives. They got scars, surfed the big waves, scaled the cliffs. They were growers. They were dealers. They were stoned. Abandoned and feared. Desperate for connection, for freedom, for family. For belonging.

It was all true.

Racer, the lankiest of them, was working on a surfboard blank in the makeshift shaping bay installed under the house in Monaco Street. His hand white with fibreglass dust, carefully guided a rip of sandpaper along the length of the rails before caressing the pristine surface. His sinewy limbs were always the first thing noticed about him, and with his protective face mask, he looked like a praying mantis. Some would say he moved at the same speed. He would spend weeks shaping one surfboard, but this was nothing to do with his sloth like pace, it was his strong work ethic. He was a born craftsman.

One side of the workshop didn't have a wall and was exposed to the ignored side yard of the house. It was sealed with a sheet of clear plastic, taped to the house frame. The plastic sheeting could barely breathe under the film of fibreglass dust and the smell of resin that cut the air. It filtered the hot sunlight as it punched in from the west. The opposite wall of the shaping bay had the advantage of a solid wall which connected it to the main house. The length of the wall was fixed with racks, displaying a quiver of surfboard blanks hand labelled with their future riders names Tora, Oli, Skinny, Jay, Racer, Frankie, Muzza and Digga.

Magazines were crudely dissected and stuck to the wall above the workbench. There were pictures of idolised bikini models and local girls who had made it to the hallowed pages of Penthouse. Wow, there were a few. Racer's favourite was Samantha. A brunette, thin as a whip, with pert breasts, pierced nipples that grazed the sunlight and a tumbling wave of ebony hair. In Racer's humble opinion, the best Penthouse page of her was the one where she was playing with a handheld shower nozzle on the back of a superyacht. The way she was captured, guiding that water jet onto her pussy like it was the best thing that had ever happened to her, was pure art, and she understood art. Speaking of Samantha's pussy, rumour had it that she crashed her brand new Honda (that she bought with her Penthouse money) when her pussy got stuck under the brake peddle. *Don't drive with cats, babe,* Racer thought each time he gazed at her black curls. As engaging as the torn out pages were, the pride of place on the shaping bay wall was reserved for feature articles about Tora Jones, *Ex-Pro Surfer* and godhead of the house.

The very youngest tenant of 1991 Monaco Street was Oli. He was a runaway from Dee Why in Sydney. He was no more than fifteen but looked eleven, with his flossy white hair sitting atop his olive skinned frame, like a ball of luminous silken thread. He was a sensitive child, until there was a surfboard under his arm.

They said he was a mean surfer, ruthless on the waves and had a hell of an appetite for winning.

'Dude! Racer? China's here for his stuff!'
Oli shouted from upstairs.

'Hang on man!' Racer, not at all ready for China's arrival.

Racer finished, hung his face mask and moved to the workbench that was completely covered in mismatched objects. It was a landing pad for things that had no place.

Nobody knew why he was called China. He was hard to find out on the streets, and when out in the surf, the others, even the wolves and hungry dogs, would give him all the waves he wanted, except for Tora. Tora didn't have to make room for anybody, and it was ironic that that's all he ever did. Legend had it that China was the best surfer the Gold Coast had seen, before Tora of course. The girls would gush about China like he was some kind of unicorn. His hair was unthinkably straight and golden. It was long. The longest it could be. All the way down his back, tied up like a Palomino's tail. He wasn't too tall, or too bulky, but he moved like a panther. To add to his mystical reputation, he grew an impressively long beard. It was blonde, naturally, and covered his face with so much intent that nobody knew what he really looked like.

This was the third foil Racer had sold in the last few hours. It was Sunday afternoon after all. Every Sunday, starting at four, Island Dreams nightclub, down on

Beach Road, opened its doors for a flurry of youthful abandon. Patrons would arrive in throngs and thongs, fresh from an afternoon of drinking and live music down at the wharf. The posters hollered seductive rhymes. Girls would sip Midori and Cokes and West Coast Coolers in their bikinis and sundresses. The boys would drink anything they could get their hands on. They were so ripped and on the prowl for something more, someone to hold, but not too much more, just enough to get them through the night. Some guys couldn't even wait to get their catch home and would only get as far as the soft dark dunes. No need to complicate things.

Racer stiffly opened the metal drawer that rested low under the heaving workbench. The squeaking rollers were grinding together with rust, unwilling to open without a scream. Racer pulled out a small brown paper bag bulging with the biggest asset in the house. He dipped his hand into the bag and extracted several small foil packages. He selected one and unwrapped it to survey the contents. He inspected the weed, homegrown and fragrant, and rewrapped it before China abruptly entered the shaping bay. China was clutching a twenty dollar note and slapped it on the bench before swiftly pocketing the foil Racer had just extracted from the stash. China looked behind him, as if expecting somebody.

'Where's Jay?'
'Island Dreams.'
'Little fuck owes me. Tora 'round?'

'Nope.'

'Give us two more, on Jay,' China sniggered.

'Fuck off man.'

China snatched the whole bag of grass. 'What ya gonna do? Tell Tora?'

China laughed outrageously, insanely, as he tucked the bag into the waistband of his faded board shorts. With that, he chuckled one more time while adjusting his tail and left the workshop without another word. Defeated, Racer stopped himself from reacting to the theft. He knew better, and Tora was always kept in the dark about the roaring household drug trade—it needed to stay that way, nobody wanted to end up in the *boardroom* with him. Jay would have to watch his own back.

To be called to the *boardroom* when shit went down, and Tora was involved, was a serious matter and only happened once in a blue moon. Nobody forgot. With the La Quinta boys, duelling took place out the back, in the surf—in the *boardroom*. Jay was always up for it, he loved the fighting and the spectacle and was often calling it or summoned there, usually when Tora was out of town. It was hard to fight out there on surfboards, regardless of what the waves were doing. It was a question of gravity and how much of a pounding one could take from fist and wave. The rules; no weapons just your surfboard, no leg rope and the best of three waves threw first punch. Both parties always came back, but when Tora called it, without fail something was broken at first strike—board, bone, tooth, reputation, pride. Tora was the tiger. Unchallenged, unquestioned.

CHAPTER FOUR

Come As You Are

The nightclub entrance always looked strange in the late afternoon half-light. That moment when a wash of greyness takes hold, before the night, and covers the day's imperfections with a nervous sleight of hand. Filthy and crawling with stories nobody wanted to hear, the corridor was claustrophobic and more like a holding cell for all those eager bodies who craved access past the metal swinging door. As if there was a need to advertise, there was a fluorescent yellow and blue poster which preciously sat in a glass cabinet fixed to the black bruised wall. *Island Dreams: Sunday Arvo! Come As You Are! $1 Drinks For The Ladies!* peddling its wares.

There were three blonde girls in pink tube dresses trying to get past Gina the Door Bitch. Gina didn't like the daylight hours. She couldn't be bothered with this trio of under-aged musk sticks. *You can sell all you like, but you're not charming me,* Gina thought loudly as she turned the girls away, again, for the third Sunday in a row.

The interior walls throbbed. The club was in full swing and smelled like a smoke grenade. There were salty surfer girls in high cut swimsuits, drinking their green drinks and laughing, loud. The sea dogs were smoking hot in their board shorts, faded tee shirts and matted hair. The rest of the crowd was a rough mix of has-been beauties, drifters and shady businessmen who simply enjoyed the spectacle and the tipsy ladies. Those dollar drinks were a hit.

Ash, heavy eyed and faded, made her way backstage and into the vacant dressing room. At least she had some paying work tonight. She was one of the regular models for Ravaged Swimwear, a local bikini brand that was the Holy Grail for up and coming local models. All the girls wanted to work for Ravaged. Ash was quick to realise that modelling swimwear in this town was one of the most respectable positions a girl could have. Adoring fans, newspaper appearances, job offers with promotional agencies and even invitations onto superyachts to serve drinks to men in white shoes. Not ideal for Ash, but she was equipped and getting hungry. Ash thought about her Mother, and the eternal disappointment she delivered her. *'Here comes the over-educated skate-bum slash artist,'* Joan Smith would say, ever since Ash appeared on the cover of that magazine, SKTR. That was a year ago.

Defeated, Ash dropped her bag on the bench and shuffled into the gritty bathroom. No matter where she was, or the circumstance of her life, Ash found great solace in a warm shower. The tiny droplets almost sympathetic, as they rolled down her body, worked hard to wash away the sorrow. She ran the water hot, with a desire to cleanse it all away; expel Edie's death and the snowball that followed. Leaving home had been a split decision. She chose not to call it running away, but in reality, she knew that's exactly what she did. She ran away, thinking she could escape something insurmountable. Under the steaming bullets of water, the remaining black make-up ran down her face as she finally released the pain. With a surge of grief, a ball of lead seemed to leave her chest with a jolt. *Was that my heart actually breaking?* Ash started to sob. There was a wash of emotion as if everything had hit her for the first time. She leaned against the back wall of the shower and sank down in despair, naked and shuddering with tears.

Jay walked along Beach Road towards Island Dreams. He preferred arriving alone instead of with the pack in case he changed his mind at the last minute. Island Dreams was a Pandora's Box for Jay. He'd been there a hundred times, and each time was an event. Fucking or fighting was the usual outcome, and tonight he was not feeling like either. *That girl.* That girl toppled him this afternoon. *Just a drink or two, and to stay out of the house long enough to avoid Tora,* was his goal.

Jay chose the *Staff Only* entrance and swiftly entered the club. He knew Gina had grown weary of him long ago, since that night he punched the glass cabinet door to take down the poster. Best not get into the reasons.

The loud music was a force as Jay entered the club. Zoo People, the band on stage, was thrashing out a song ferociously. Johnny, the lead singer, looked like a misfit. He was Japanese and a serious-looking dude. Tall and lean with a dark demeanour, he glared at the audience as he growled into the microphone. He thumped with his voice as the tightly herded sheep slam danced.

Johnny Sato had lived on the Gold Coast for ten years. He moved from Tokyo when his Father bought a golf course in the early eighties. Johnny was used to being an outsider. Being an outsider amongst outsiders worked best for him. He lived to his own rhythm, God knows he could afford to. Johnny only spoke when he had something to say. He truly believed actions spoke louder than words and was sure to live by this golden rule. Johnny was Tora Jones' best friend. Tora spent his formative years in Japan with his Mother Myrtle Jones, a highly respected news correspondent, before he returned to Australia at twenty years old. Johnny and Tora first met at Narita Airport. A flight-delay before heading back to Australia was the conduit. Johnny had Tora upgraded to First Class so they could continue their conversation across the Pacific. The pair drank Suntory and smiles all the way home.

Jay worked himself into the motley crowd before he passed his housemate Oli who was with a mousey looking girl called Emma. He'd made an early catch, although, in Jay's opinion, could've done better if he waited just a little longer. Emma looked like low hanging fruit.

'Hey. Tora here?' Jay enquired, trying to appear nonchalant.

'Hey man. Nah, he split. He's got that early flight.'
'Today ripped!'
'Yeah. For sure.'

Deeper into the crowd, Jay felt assured he wouldn't be running into Tora tonight. He was used to avoiding consequences, ducking and weaving from forces greater than himself, just to buy another day. He'd learnt that from his Dad.

Ash emerged from the shower feeling more relaxed. Less volcanic. She slowly dried herself off before taking on the arduous task of preparing her mane in time for the show. Swimwear parades were easy money, if one could stomach it. All Ash had to do was go out onto the stage a few times in a bikini. Skip out, wave her arms, a little hop, a little twirl, wiggle her ass for a moment. When she felt the guys had screamed sufficiently, she pranced off the stage like a show pony with its tail high in the air. *'Quit while you're hot, and make room for the next girl!'* her boss chanted as she clapped her hands together, as if explaining to infants, *'Leave them salivating.'*

Zoe was an original Ravaged model, a veteran. She looked like she had an American Southern drawl, but she didn't. Well endowed with curves to die for, her copper ponytail lingered around her pearl throat like feathers, and her glittered shoulders moved sensually as she murmured sweet sentiments. Her bright eyes, a luxurious shade of emerald, made her look like she was in a constant state of ecstasy. She had a pout that made all the local girls green with envy, and if they weren't destroyed already, an ass that could set off sirens. She was from Logan and they all resented that.

Ash was having a tangerine bikini top tied by Zoe, who was standing bare-breasted before the Hollywood mirrors. Showgirl erotica shone back as Ash glimpsed at their sizzling reflection. Since day one on the Coast, Zoe had been Ash's rock. Ever helpful, she noticed Ash had been crying. She gently inquired as she adjusted Ash's bikini by pulling the Brazilian pants higher and narrower, over the crest of her bottom.

'Perfect. Are you nervous?'
'I'm fine.'

Hiding her doubts, Ash stiffly smiled and applied her lip gloss, again.

'What happened today? How was the shoot? Did you find somewhere to stay?'
'No, I didn't. I'm really sorry Zoe, can I spend one more night at your place?'
'Oh, I don't know Ash. Maggie is getting pretty anxious about extra people in her place. There's a hostel just up my street, pretty sweet place I think. They close early though. Don't miss that last bus.'

Ash responded with a warm look, trying to appear understanding. She jumped subjects as she looked into Zoe's eyes, reflected in the mirror.

'When do we get paid?'
'End of the month.'

'Now go out there and show 'em who's boss! Hey, you look great,' Zoe tapped Ash's tangerine behind.

The music changed to something more bouncy. Ash moved toward the side of the stage to wait for her queue. She adjusted her posture and further elongated her slender body for a moment.

Johnny exited the stage and paused as he brushed past Ash in slow motion. Their eyes met. Johnny looked at her with an assessing gaze, expressionless. Ash was taken aback by his intense eyes. His face completely closed. He continued into the dressing room, soon followed by his drummer who had a helmet of red hair and a body like a drought stricken tree branch.

'What do ya mean I played too loud?' he cried, following Johnny through the dressing room with a contorted face.

Johnny didn't turn to acknowledge him. Instead he held up the drumsticks and snapped them like twigs. The stunned drummer, with his flailing arms, almost dove to the floor to retrieve his sticks. Johnny stood and watched, without amusement.

Ash skipped onto the stage. She felt almost lifted by the roar of the crowd as she pranced on her toes under the spotlight. She couldn't see the whistling crowd for the brightness, nor the game show host inspired disc jockey who loudly announced her appearance.

'Introducing Ash! Modelling this tiny bikini by Ravaged Swimwear! Thank you, Ash! Hope you're loving Surfers because Surfers loves you!' he blared.

Jay was in the crowd, like a stone. He was mesmerised by the vision of her. The hypnotic sway of her body and the swing of her hair was enough to floor him. The guys around Jay were cheering while he was paralysed. His guard was down, and his seawolf instincts were curled up tight in his heart as he rushed through tactics. Ash disappeared from the spotlight and Zoe took it.

Backstage, Ash prepared to leave the club. She undressed and put her new tangerine bikini in her shoulder bag. They were part of the payment. *Foreign currency a month ago*, she mused. Ash knew she had to hurry. That last bus had a reputation for running on its own ghost schedule. One night at the hostel wasn't going to kill her. Ash had made peace with the idea. Besides, she had a job trial tomorrow at Cult Kitchen, the most hip cafe on the Coast, so onwards and upwards. Ash worked her way into the crowd to leave.

Jay saw Ash making her way through the club, heading for the door, and soon she escaped his view. He was closed in by waves of dancing and drinking revellers. Jay started to push through with desperation to catch up to her.

'Hey! Hey, Ash!' he shouted out to a deaf room.

Oblivious to Jay's attempts, Ash carried on through as the seas parted, leading her to a swift exit. Jay continued to call out and push forward until his elbow took aim at the wrong target. China, less than impressed by Jay's gouge and even less impressed to see Jay out in the club with a Corona in his hand, grabbed Jay by the shoulder.

'You! Where's my fifty bucks?' China growled closely in his ear.

'What fifty?' Jay foolishly claimed.

Jay's question was answered loud and clear with a punch. Jay was down. Ash was gone. China moved on.

Ash briskly walked up to the beach end of the road toward the bus stop. The crested street exhaled silently under the glossy full moon, as it was cleansed of the day. The night seemed later than ten. Sunday nights were sleepy in this town unless you lived the Island Dreams routine.

Time seemed to crawl while Ash waited under the intermittent fluorescent light. She recalled the last time she felt such awful light blanket her aura—that green hospital waiting room. At least the outcome of that was some decisive action. Indeed, Ash reflected, she needed more decisive action now, as she sat self abandoned in the bus shed.

Crashing through Ash's despondency, a car full of drunks zoomed past. One of the men was wolf-whistling at her, half hanging out the window. A bottle was thrown, and the amber glass rained onto the street. With the small explosion, like a wake-up call, Ash realised she had missed the last bus. She looked to the sky in despair. More time passed, and the street fell back to sleep.

'Are you okay?'

Jay stood in the middle of the street, flawless, in the halo of shattered glass. Ash glanced at him and looked up towards the sky once more, hoping her tears would not roll.

'You missed the last bus.'
'I think so,' she agreed to the sky.

Ash moved off the bench and sat down on the curb to escape the horrible light. Defeated, she was playing with the straps of her bag, which contained all of her possessions. She was well aware she had nowhere to go from this moment, and avoided eye contact with the sun bleached Samaritan.

Jay's thumping heart and racing mind were not helping him appear calm and collected. His interior was too loud for the task at hand. He knew that with a girl like this, there's only one chance. Like approaching a fawn in the forest, he crept forward trying not to startle her. He carefully sat down beside Ash, crushingly slow. He held his breath as if his life depended on it. Ash didn't react since she was busy with her own distraction of trying to hide she was rock bottom. She weighed up her options internally, and finally somehow out of rhythm with the moment, she tried to speak, but... nothing.

'Can I take you somewhere? I can take you anywhere you want,' he whispered.
'No.' Ash mouthed.

There was an extended silence. The moon kept shining, and the squawk of a plover rang out from the nearby park. Looking in opposite directions, lost for words, Ash and Jay both felt undeniable energy between them. So fragile. Jay finally dared to speak.

'I saw you at the club.' No, clumsy. He paused.
'How's that rock star dude? When he dropped
the mic and grabbed the drummer's sticks?'
'Yeah I saw you there,' she tried to lift her voice
in kindness. 'No, I didn't see that, but I saw him snap
them like a maniac.'
'Hah, it's not the first time.'

Jay leaned slightly sideways toward Ash. His fingers touched hers and she breathed a sigh, then a small laugh, as she looked to the sky for support. They enjoyed the quiet as the furrow between them disappeared and gently whispered their small talk, without eye contact. Soon they decided to walk. Anywhere.

CHAPTER FIVE

Welcome To The Jungle

The ice was broken and a new curve had swung the path for Ash and Jay. They stepped crisply onto the rain-popped sand and walked together, languidly toward midnight. The lights disappeared from the bordering highrises, making room for the stars above. The moon was less enthusiastic now as she sat high above, all seeing, all knowing. Ash quietly considered the moon as the *dues ex machina* of the human story, because surely we'll all be asking for a miraculous solution at some point.

The black sky and the black sea became one, only to meet its end at the white lapping waves that crept onto the silver sand in tufts. The sea innocently pulled the beach inwards, inch by inch, attempting to satisfy the insatiable tide. Ash felt invigorated, nervous and actually happy. Even if it was a fleeting moment, it was more than enough tonight. Tonight was all she needed. A small fracture in her despair, making way for a shimmer of light. Ash felt close to Jay; maybe the sensation was heightened because she hadn't felt close to anybody in the longest time. Nobody had held her, caressed her sadness or tenderly lifted her chin with their sympathetic hand. She was left to cajole her own tears into retreat.

Changing pace, Jay peeled off his moth-eaten tee shirt and casually enquired, 'Have you ever swam in the surf at night?'

As dark as it was, Ash couldn't take her eyes off Jay's bare torso. Now without a shirt and his worn out board shorts barely hanging on, she suddenly realised what she was dealing with. This guy was going to swallow her up. Eat her whole. She knew her weaknesses and feared them, she also knew she had impulses when it came to boys like this. Ash looked at the tattoos that were engraved in smokey green on his perfectly rounded corners.

'Oh, my God. This one is just like a drawing I did. That's so weird,' she dared to reach out and touch a tattoo on his shoulder.
'You draw? Cool... Where ya from?'

Jay seemed a bit embarrassed. He paused to look closely at her face, and he tensed again as he remembered the little fawn he was dealing with. The nuance of her mouth curling just before she spoke destroyed him.

'Oh, you wouldn't know it. It's down south of Sydney. In the Southern Highlands. It's nothing like here. Black Ridge.'
'Geez, that's a big move,' Jay gawked.
'I suppose.'

Jay turned and started walking with Ash again. He momentarily forgot about his swim and his discarded tee fifty meters back, as he immersed himself in her.

'I've been here for as long as I can remember. We moved heaps, but always round here. Why'd ya move?'

'Fresh start. What better place?' Ash swung her arms wide to the horizon of low towers that huddled behind the evening dunes.

'It's a hard place to leave.'

Without warning, Jay took off, running into the black waves and out of sight. Ash's smile faded after a few moments of not being able to see him. She started to walk closer to the shoreline with the cold froth bubbling and dragging beneath her feet. She could see nothing but white peaks intermittently catching the distant moonlight. Ash was panicked to the core; she was trembling. Jay had disappeared, and it felt like an eternity. She stood in the shallows clutching her bag and scanning the darkness. She wanted to cry. She felt as though she had left her body, observing her panic, realising it was pure irrational fear. Then she heard him and all the blood returned to her face in a flush of warmth. Joy rose to her mouth.

'Yew!' he cried, loud enough for the whole beach.

Ash turned to see Jay triumphantly running towards her. More visible, the closer he got, she could see he was in his element, dripping and almost naked—if it wasn't for those tattered board shorts that were ready to come right off. As Jay approached Ash, he could see she was upset. He was exhilarated, his body shimmered and she reached out to touch his wet heart with her cold palm.

'What's wrong?' he asked.

Ash was unable to say anything reasonable to him, so she chose silence. Instead, she took hold of his wrist and guided him closer to her. Face to face, Jay caught his breath and held himself dangerously close to her body. She didn't retract. She stood firm, not cowering from the intensity of the moment. She wanted him. She took him and kissed him. Ash was no fawn.

His heart shaped mouth must have been the softest thing about him. This was the tenderness Ash craved. She kissed him decadently like she'd known him forever, deeply and unreserved. He responded in a way that surged a blind force through her. Everything lit up for Ash as Jay let go of some precious restraint. The only obvious thing to do next, in Ash's racing mind, was to guide him down onto the sand before straddling his wet hips.

When she could feel his pulsing body beneath her, she knew they shared undeniable chemistry. It was the only tension release Ash could afford. Physical satis-faction was an immediate priority. Ash's curtain of hair shrouded them from the outside world as they kissed, leaving nothing between them but a thin mist of sea air. Her baby pink claws sunk into his hard shoulders, savagely raising the stakes. The waves crashed behind them and a distant siren called. Ash gripped his body with all of hers and he knew the hunt was over. A delicious struggle was to ensue. He wanted to take her home, and feast, forever.

The darkness settled around them as the moment calmed. Jay put the brakes on and revisited his tactics to get her home. Entwined on the sand, he warmly stroked her hair as she draped her body over his.

'I lost my sister, and people keep on telling me that life goes on, but for me, that's the saddest part. I know there is no happy ending because now my parents are stuck there, and so I'm in this stupid, shitty ending. I'm looking for my happy start,' she placed a whispered kiss on his attentive ear. 'I needed this move, it felt like my last chance.'

Jay closed his eyes in search of words. He felt empty of the kind of words she needed. He wanted to speak of love and sex and eternity. He wanted to speak the most beautiful words, but they escaped him.

'I'm sorry,' Jay wiped the hair that crossed her face. 'I know it feels like you're never going to see the sunshine, ever again. But you will... and you will by spending time with people who care about you. I learnt this from living without my Mum.'

Ash pulled herself upright, still pinning him with her slender bronze thighs. Her shirt now wet from pressing onto his skin, clung to her. She looked into his eyes and tentatively shared a hopeful smile.

'Yeah. Okay. Show me sunshine,' her voice barely audible over the sea.

Jay had a devilish grin which gave Ash sparks. He hesitantly released his sensual grip of her sandy legs and raised himself onto his elbows. *Thinking.* He looked over toward the distant beach car park.

'Let's go to my place. It's not that far.'

Ash accepted, it was a saviour, at least for tonight. They walked through the deserted beachside car park outside the surf club. It was often full of holiday maker's station wagons and cars left there for a few days by residents of the crowded beach towers nearby.

'I know I parked my car around here somewhere,' Jay scanned the sleepy car park. 'Ahh, there she is!'

Jay approached a white Toyota Corolla with shopping trolley dents and a box of tissues in the back window.

'Just go around the other side. My door gets jammed, I'll just be a sec.'

The car door wasn't opening, and Jay calmly held Ash's gaze while his hands were doing all the work. After a few moments, Jay cracked open the door and jumped into the car hurriedly. There was more fidgeting before the engine kicked to life. A kitsch mirror ornament of a white rabbit lasted about two seconds before Jay pulled it down and thrust it under the driver's seat. Ash waited to be let into the passenger side, amused that he was so disorganised.

Immediately, Ash realised *Avalon* was playing in soft crumbling sound bytes. She turned up the radio, just a little.

'My sister loved this song so much!' Ash beamed. 'Umm... Oh yeah.'

Jay had no idea what song this was. He remained distracted as he fumbled to reverse the car and pulled out of the car park, bumping the wipers and going too heavy on the brakes. He was not a natural and obviously out of his element.

'Ahh, this old baby has a mind of her own.'

Ash smirked and looked away. They drove the beachside streets without speaking. Ash was immersed in the song and was enchanted by the aura of sea mist that pooled around each street light they passed.

'What about your Dad?'
'He's local but he moves around a lot. Kinda in trouble all the time,' Jay laughed.
'You seem to handle it well.'
'Yeah. I guess. I had help from a mate. He's like a big brother. I've lived at his place since—Shit, petrol.'
'I just saw a servo back there,' Ash suggested.
'Nah, my place is just a couple of blocks away on Monaco Street, let's walk.'

Jay pulled over, bumping the curb. Still barefoot and shirtless, and Ash, sandy and exhausted, they got out of the car and started walking. They soon arrived at a sprawling seventies Spanish style house. The white rendered archways were camouflaged by dried out palm throngs and tracts of long-dead vines. The house had a matching concrete letterbox that was half broken. 1991. The large front window adjacent to the front door was central to the house and faced the wide street.

They crossed the front yard toward the side of the house, overstepping beer bottles. There was a snapped skateboard, and an old bike with the front wheel bent in half, which blocked the side entrance. The house was dark.

'Watch your step,' Jay warned.

'That skateboard has seen better days,' Ash was amused.

'Oh yeah... my fault, I'm always breaking stuff.'

They continued through the shrouded landscape and around the corner of the house. A dog's bark bellowed from inside.

'Shuddup, Moose!' a muffled voice snapped.

Jay took hold of a ladder fixed to the side of the house. The old white concrete rendering was busy and laid thick, it reminded Ash of icing on a wedding cake.

'Welcome to *La Quinta!* Now get that ass of yours up to the penthouse,' Jay playfully motioned towards the rooftop, not too high above.

Ash was quietly laughing as she climbed the ladder in the dark. To her, it seemed outrageously fun. Jay climbed through the window first, then he helped Ash climb into the room, stepping on Jay's single bed. Jay flicked a lamp on which threw a low, red glow onto the bed. The room was small and crammed with Jay's belongings. Ash scanned the room and paused to look at a large Rollins Band poster pinned to the yellow wallpaper. They both gazed at it for too long.

Jay broke the silence, 'You ever seen 'em live? I first saw them here a couple of summers ago, and then they came back to town a few months ago. Henry Rollins blew my mind.'

'Henry? No. I've never heard of them, there's this band called Nirvana. I think they're coming to the wharf on Australia Day. Should be alright, I guess.'

'Uhuh. Maybe. Rollins Band is best loud. Tomorrow I'll crank it up for ya.'

'So that's the next bit of sunshine you're gonna show me?' Ash was being kittenish.

Jay stepped closer to Ash and held both her hands tightly. 'No, this is.'

He moved in fast and passionately kissed her neck that glowed flamingo pink under the rose lamp. His wholesome kiss turned into a gentle bite. After a brief hesitation, Ash engaged and put her arms firmly around his broad naked shoulders and tenderly kissed the salt from his warm skin. Jay reached down and pulled the sandy bedsheets back before he guided her with his mouth down onto the narrow bed. His weight pressed on every inch of her as she anticipated his next move. He grabbed the pillow from beneath her head and tossed it to the floor. Kneeling in-between her legs, she gasped as he pulled her roughly toward him with strong and confident authority. After a few moments, Jay lifted the sheets over their heads, cocooning them for the first time.

'You're so beautiful. I wanna hold you tight forever,' he barely whispered.

She was now in his world, a cotton cave for two. He kissed her mouth, exploring with his hands the elegant stretch of her torso. He softly brushed her hair aside, and then her clothing. His mouth followed his decisive hands, and he feasted on Ash until the first bird announced the day, briskly and unapologetic. That was the last thing Ash remembered before she fell asleep in his grip. She felt captured, like a fawn under a bear paw and she didn't mind.

CHAPTER SIX

I'm The One

Ash woke up before Jay. Sunlight giddily crept across the yellow wallpaper of his bedroom as the Bangalow palms swayed outside. Their midsummer violet bloom and crimson berries fed the squabbling lorikeets that had unceremoniously encroached on the backyard. Her eyes searched Jay's bedroom for clues. The lemon walls were plastered with surf and music posters. Clothes were lying around amongst one broken surfboard and one intact. Ash wondered if the wilting plant on the overladen desk was dying from a lack of water or absence of light, and *why not help it if you saw it suffering?* She never understood how dying plants could go unassisted right under their guardian's nose. Although small, it was to her, a sign of poor character, capable of witnessing a slow death without intervention. Well, that's how it would be seen where she was from.

She watched Jay's handsome face and flawless body breathe in their shared morning air. Ash slid out of bed like a sly cat, not wanting Jay to stir. *The morning after is so confronting,* she thought. Ash felt shy and wanted to avoid awkward chat—she really needed to find the bathroom without delay. She found her bikini and sundress and silently slipped into them without disturbing the atmosphere of the room. Carefully, she opened the bedroom door and crossed the threshold into a whole new world. She was inside La Quinta.

The upstairs hallway was long and luminous. Most of the light was coming from a doorway opposite Jay's room. Ash stepped forward to see what lay ahead and paused to take in the new scene. The bedroom seemed unoccupied. Compared to Jay's quarters, the spacious room was impossibly organised and smelled like peeled mandarin. It was the enormous master bedroom of the old mansion, reclining in silence.

Ash imagined that sometime ago, the master bedroom would have exuded glamour with new peach coloured carpet so deep, one may lose a pearl earring in it. The walls masked with decadent silver geometric wallpaper, would have quaintly diffused the evening glow of a chandelier which dangled notoriously over an oval apricot and maple waterbed made for sex.

La Quinta, had become a tattered whore of a house. At twenty years old, she was filled with scads of orifices for young men's insatiable desires and was the shame of Monaco Street.

Ash measured her quiet steps into the bedroom that

was left humbly sparse by its tenant. The well curated contents seemed oddly attuned to a parallel universe, one that had a sense of purity. Ash knew already that this room must be the sanctuary of the house, gated invisibly, and left to absorb its own radiance. She wondered about its owner as she bravely sank into its confines.

Nearest to the door was a small wooden table, black and hand-carved. Upon it rested a bonsai tree that looked gnarled and twisted from years of hard pruning. It was probably older than the massive oak tree that was now Edie's vigilant keeper. At the foot of the tiny mammoth was a mossy undergrowth with the daintiest flowers, lime and delightful, reaching up to graze on the morning light. On the facing wall, there was a well-used Powell Peralta skateboard with scuffed edges and candy red trim. Its yellow Rat Bones wheels were bright like birthday party jelly beans against the peeling silver wallpaper. The skateboard was carefully placed with nothing within reach of it, like a religious monument. *Rightly so,* Ash agreed.

Further along the wall, bookshelves hovered all the way up its heights. The books were few but perfectly arranged, like an expensive bookstore. Their rows were occasionally interrupted by relics of tastefull random selection. A volcanic rock. A butter coloured candle. A horse conch seashell. An antique globe. A crystal whisky decanter. A Buddha with a Mona Lisa smile, entwined in a Rudraksha mala.

A double bed lay tightly in the corner, stripped back

to perfect white, abandoned somehow. With this, Ash realised she had been lost in the moment and took a long step back to exit the grand bedroom.

The distant sound of a heavy door closing activated a loud rumbling outside. Ash approached the large hallway window that was blanketed with tired ochre drapes, that should have been mothballed years ago. She pulled them aside only slightly to see where the rough noise was coming from. She now had a clear view of La Quinta's long front yard that was littered with discarded toys of juvenile desire.

A man was leaving the house with a carry bag and, curiously, a snowboard. He sauntered like he was in the Wild West, dressed in black, head to toe. There was a calmness about him, the way he moved, that made everything hold a curious stillness. The lorikeets stopped squabbling, and the marigolds turned their faces to the sun. The cosmic sea parted for this mysterious man, as he wandered up the driveway to meet his chariot, a menacing black car with a skull and crossbones on the hood.

Ash wanted to know what his face looked like. She wondered if he slept in that master bedroom. He slipped into the mean-looking car, and the throb of the engine ricocheted up the street as it pulled away. Two swallows darted towards the window, playing in the golden air, while, out of nowhere, the ancient scent of frankincense and myrrh charged the hall.

'Tora,' a crystalline female voice breathed into Ash's un-expecting ear. 'For you, he is everywhen,' the canorous words trickled down Ash's spine. 'My beloved is mine, and I am his, he feedeth among the lilies until the day break, and the shadows flee away,' she continued, barely audible.

With tingling skin, Ash turned to the young woman who was standing very close behind. She was waiting to be seen. Ash was stunned by the ethereal girl, with eyes that crackled like green cellophane and lips like fronds of pink succulent. Tresses of hair fell over her torso, the colour of wood apple jam. When Ash glanced downward, she tried not to appear prudish in her expression, realising the woman was blindingly naked. Before Ash could remember how to speak, the girl turned and walked toward the staircase lightly and without a sound. Ash's mouth turned dry. She started to follow the strange girl, but then stopped when she saw there were three guys uncomfortably asleep on the landing of the over-sized, curved staircase. The girl carelessly stepped over them. Nobody stirred.

Ash hesitated again before she went further to explore the half-lit house. She just wanted to find the bathroom. In an effort to encapsulate her anxiety, she held her breath as she overstepped the sleeping trio. Ash heard voices downstairs. She walked into the lounge room which was, as expected, expansive and beyond repair. The walls built with cinnamon coloured brick, offered dark archways leading to other places and corridors.

They were bare, except for dusty clamshell light fittings that glowed ominously in the obscure setting.

Ash's eyes grew as big as saucers at the sight of the young woman who was now lying face down on the couch, tranquil and perfectly still. She had luminous skin, like Mother of Pearl, and her hair spiderwebbed across her back. Her curls were set ablaze with colour by the electric clamshell overhead. The girl reclined in the hungover room among the bongs, empty beer bottles and full ashtrays, as if she was elsewhere. She had the grace of a time travelling Renaissance nude, Ash observed with a sorry face.

At the other end of the long couch, that Ash assumed was made for swingers, Oli and Racer sat, slumped with lazy smiles. They momentarily paused their discussion and glanced up at Ash without fixing their gaze, as if she too, was invisible to them.

'Yeah, I wanna go down to Nimbin, ay? Skinny has been cleanin up from his surfin' sponsor. He wants to come'n get a heapa mull. Volcanic soil there ay... wicked heads man. Fuckin' wicked. I'm starving,' Oli drooled.
'Yeah, starvin' heaps,' Racer giggled softly like an infant with his eyes closed.

Ash could only think about finding the bathroom and couldn't get out of the lounge room fast enough. She chose the nearest dark archway to disappear into and finally found it. Filthy beyond anything she had expected, the bathroom had a broken mirror, beer bottles all over the vanity unit, and a bathtub that resembled an abandoned cup of tea. Ash rinsed her face with cool relief and studied her cracked reflection. She ran her index finger along the sharp fracture, dulling her mood. A change of heart about the ravenous seawolf washed over her. She took one of the empty beer bottles and filled it with water and carried it out of the bathroom.

Ash returned to the staircase and carefully stepped over the sleeping men on the landing. She noticed that one had a blue swallow tattooed on each side of his neck, just like the pair that flew towards the hall window moments before—when the naked girl spoke her riddle. The sleepers didn't stir. Ash moved back through the house until she reached the vacant master bedroom.

Kneeling down to look at the bonsai tree, Ash touched its leaves with fondness before pouring water lightly onto its delicate soil. It reminded her of Edie somehow. Ash found it enchanting, how the sunlight caught the water droplets, in miniature scale. The sun was high now, and she walked towards the window and gazed down into the disbanded front yard. She found herself reflecting on the man she saw out there earlier and turned to scan the room one last time. Ash picked up the skateboard and admired it, brashly giving it an expert spin in her hands and then gently put it back before being distracted by the other artefacts. There were magazines piled on the floor under a cricket ball sized quartz crystal. She picked it up and held it high in the sun's ray to see the coloured light refract inside.

She closed her eyes as if to breathe in the room and the energy it seemed to give her. Ash looked down to see that one of the well thumbed magazines, SKTR, had her picture on the cover and was shyly amused. She replaced the crystal carefully back on top of her glossy, happy, one dimensional face. Ash smirked when she realised she had touched everything within reach attentively, as if meeting a lover for the very first time. It was not in her nature to go into a stranger's bedroom, let alone start touching everything. She felt welcome.

Ash tip-toed across the hall and entered Jay's room, which now had a block of daylight threatening to wake him. She grabbed her bag, ready for a quick exit, and wrote a note using a page out of her worn sketchbook.

Thanks for the sunshine. x

Stealth, Ash glided up the hall with her cotton shoulder bag swaying. Her rose petal toenails dug into the swirls of ancient aquamarine carpet as she swiftly approached the stairs that lead to La Quinta's main entrance.

And just like that, she was out.

CHAPTER SEVEN

Time After Time

The September heat started to rise on the highway as the beastly black car snarled its way north, toward the international airport. Tora was going to Japan for a few months, as he did each year, to spend time with his Mother Myrtle Jones, and refine his skills on the slopes, if he stayed in the country long enough. He would usually stay through to the other side of Christmas, naturally Myrtle loved that.

Johnny had owned the Ford Falcon XB since he arrived in Australia ten year ago, back in 81'. His Father had bestowed it, along with a Miami Beach penthouse, with the explanation it had been given to him by somebody that was indebted to the Sato family. The Beast had become something of a gang's lair, one with bucket seats, a massive sound system plus a sunroof. The gang only included Johnny and Tora, and that was enough.

Johnny and Tora always kept their music intake simple when fanging up the highway. It was either going to be *Faith No More, Pearl Jam* or *The Ramones*. Johnny preferred to work in three's. Only three cassettes allowed in the car at any given time. It kept the discussion to a minimum, just how they liked it. Johnny would rotate the selection each week. On this day, he had queued up *Faith No More* for the early haul to the departure lounge. The music climbed from the speakers with a pleasing vibration, and then out the tinted windows, leaving a screaming trail behind. Tora, deep in contemplation for most of the album, finally hit *stop*.

'Those dudes are trashing my house, and Jay's selling weed. Again! And who know's what else! Man... I can't take the fall for him a second time. He's gonna cost me everything,' sinking low into his black leather seat. 'I just know it.'

Johnny steadied the steering wheel with his knees as he lit a Marlboro. He habitually squinted his eyes at the same time that his lighter sparked, which was both amusing and terrifying, for even the most daring passenger.

'You gotta keep an eye on him or get rid of him,' Johnny dragged the fresh smoke into his lungs. 'Damn, he's a nightmare,' before he puffed.
'When I get back, I'm gonna clean out that place... start over,' Tora muffled as his words were vacuumed out the window.

He was like wildfire. Yeah, Tora was hot. It was his intensity that wouldn't let you look away, even if you wanted to, or needed to. His eyes, wheels of freshly chopped hazel wood, would blink slowly at the rush of the world. His left eye was his good eye. The right, ravaged by a cataract that never really healed as it should have. He couldn't see well out of it, but only Johnny knew that. Tora had a large stature but would never use it as a show of power. He was more subtle than that, he was a man of the mind. He was a sapiophile, which was the final twist in any girls knickers—wherever his travels took him. Tora had the body of an Adonis, the mind of a poet and the heart of a lion. He was thoroughly loved, all the girls agreed.

Tora quit the pro-surfing circuit when he took Jay on full time. Beyond his years, Tora had always been inclined to take on more responsibility than those around him. It was his nature. This is what had led him to this quandary with Jay. His Mother's sister, Marcy, was a foster carer and had taken on baby Jay after Nora's tragic death, all those years ago. As Jay grew into a young man, she had well and truly lost control of him. Tora, the responsible one, was somehow tasked by his adoring Mother Myrtle, and Aunt Marcy, to act as Jay's guardian from the age of fifteen, until he turned eighteen. Then, the plan was, Jay would be on his own.

Time rolled by, eventfully and painfully for Tora. Jay's eighteenth birthday came with a bang, and Tora didn't have the heart to set him out in the world. It would have left Jay destitute. Now Jay was almost twenty and Tora, at eleven years his senior, was lumped with some serious decisions to make. Tora had been suffering through his guardianship of Jay for years. He'd reached a point of feeling that it was time to clear out the nest, once and for all.

಄

Ash briskly crossed the minefield front lawn without looking back at the white wedge of a house that was set back on Monaco Street, hidden behind dead vines and overgrown sago palms. She figured Jay wouldn't even miss her this morning. Guys like *that* fucked around like nothing else. They were insatiable, or so Ash was told by all the local girls. She bet he'd made a few cry in the past.

Monaco Street was already blanketed under a dusty yellow heat haze. The parked cars crowded together like army worms along the high curb. Ash walked past Jay's petrol starved car and noticed there was a set of pretty lace doilies displayed on the rear shelf, along with that tissue box she saw. The bumper sticker for *Surfers Paradise Bowls Club* was a dead giveaway that last night, Ash was driven home in a stolen car. *This guy is something else. Criminal, yet adorable that he made such valiant efforts to get me home. Joan Smith would really sniff the onion about this, if she ever knew,* Ash pondered with a smear of sadness.

When Ash arrived at the familiar corner servo, she felt relieved to be back on the boundary of her own territory. Now it was just her versus that phone booth. The broken door wasn't going to get the better of her this morning, and this time she fought the door by holding it open with her leg and pinning it in place. She picked up the receiver and dialled the number she knew by heart. She waited patiently for an answer.

Ring... ring ... ring.

In the empty, immaculate lounge room, the Smith's phone rang its lethargic tone and remained unanswered. Disappointed, Ash hung up. Again, she picked up the receiver and dialled a number she had kept on notepaper. Ash changed her posture and forcibly smiled, hoping it would carry through in her voice. She needed to sound more upbeat than usual.

'Cult Kitchen. We grow our own,' Sam answered in a voice that made her sound like she was juggling.
'Hi Sam, it's Ash.'
'Good morning, Darl, how you going?' her tone softened. 'Nice and fresh on a Monday I see.'
'Oh yeah, I'm fine thanks. I'm going to be okay for today's trial shift,' Ash confirmed.

She was adjusting her hair and starting to relax, she could feel a new beginning rising up around her. Ash flicked her hair one more time, and caught a figure in the corner of her eye. Staring at her intently, with a baby teeth grin, was Jay. He gently tapped the window of the booth and presented a bird of paradise with a ripped stalk. For a moment, Ash was drowned with emotion and wound up her call while swallowing her visions of Edie.

'I'll see you at two. Thanks, bye.'

She hung up the phone as Jay cornered her in the booth. With his face close to hers, he handed her the flower.

'Oh... I love these.'

Ash was transported by the sight of the *strelitzia*. Jay took her by the hand and lured her to walk with him. He put his arm around her petite shoulders and passionately kissed her neck.

'I start a new job today.'

Ash was straight back into the small talk that she had spent the morning avoiding.

Jay put his distorted face to the sun. 'Let's go for a swim and hang out,' he playfully suggested.
'Yeah. Ok.'
'We'll make sure to get you there on time. Don't worry.'
'Alright, let's go,' Ash surrendered.
'Now about this sunshine...'

Jay nuzzled into Ash as she returned a half-smile, and they walked down the gentle slope of Monaco Street, back to the house.

When Ash and Jay arrived at the front yard, they were greeted by a large, rough-looking brindle Staffy, a real coffee table of a dog. He was outside sunning himself until he saw the pair and then, with a heartwarming effort, waddled to the curb while giving a yawned bark. Ash moved to meet the dog half way, slightly bowing in anticipation of the encounter.

'Don't! Moose'll eat ya up,' Jay warned, half seriously.
'Ohhh! so sweet,' Ash crouched down with the dog. 'Hi there, boy, hey Moose.'

Ash put her hand out to his muzzle and it was reciprocated with a gently calculated lick. She started to pat the dog in long affectionate strokes with the response of a furiously wagging tail.

Emma, a pasty looking young woman, sheepishly surfaced from the house carrying her scuffed high heels from the night before. Her white dress fit like an elastic band and crept up her thighs with each step she took, requiring her to adjust it several times as she hastily crossed the wide yard. Ash flashed a smile at the girl as she passed, but the girl didn't respond with any happiness. She hurried to escape the La Quinta minefield, leaving nothing behind, not even a smile.

'Ash, how'd you do this? Moose is crazy for you,' Jay marvelled. That dog hated him. 'Come, I wanna show you something inside.'

Ash followed Jay into the house, this time, they used the front door. The sizeable double entry was fixed in-between two glass panels that were textured with what looked like the base of hundreds of amber beer bottles. She followed Jay through the cinnamon bricked lounge room which housed the enormous couch. It still reminded Ash of the perfect swingers set up, maybe it was the shagpile carpet or the piles of vinyl cushions in lurid colours. There was an old television which was on, but without audience. It didn't have very good reception, offering a snowstorm with crackles of haunted gibberish. The coffee table was still covered in a mess of homemade Orchy bottle bongs, empty food wrappers, lighters, foil and a half-empty tub of grasshopper green board wax.

Ash was intrigued that the girl with the green cellophane eyes was still asleep on the couch, naked without consequence. She continued to follow Jay past the pool table and surrendered to the temptation to run her hand along the green felt that could tell a thousand stories.

'Oh wow, I haven't been near a pool table like this since I was a kid. Do you play much?'
'Yeah, but with Tora in the house, it's tough. He's a bit of a shark. Sometimes we turn it into a ping-pong table. That's heaps fun.'

Before Ash could ask Jay who Tora was, Jay continued.

'Tora's been renting this place for years, but he's hardly ever here. Always in Japan. He always helps me out... Even though I piss him off... mostly.'
'Are you related?' Ash dug deeper.
'No. I've known him since I was a kid. My foster Mum, Marcy is his Aunty... his Mum's sister. He took me in when I was fifteen,' he reflected. 'I guess I was a bit of a handful for her.'

They arrived at the back door, which was announced by a shimmering water reflection that danced up the kitchen wall toward the flaked ceiling. Ash looked out to the backyard to see a kidney shaped in-ground swimming pool, glistening perfect blue.

Jay stood beside Ash and took in the idyllic suburban view before he peeled off his shirt and somersaulted into the pool. He let himself sink to the bottom, and his golden hair looked like raw silk as it floated behind him. He seemed serene, Ash thought, and less like a seawolf. A rush of bubbles surfaced as Jay pushed back towards the edge. He stood midway along the length of the pool and extended his hand out to Ash. She touched his hand, and he fiercely grabbed her arm and pulled her swiftly into the crystal water.

'Jump in baby!' he laughed, seasoned with sarcasm that seemed to come out of nowhere.

Momentarily Ash was underwater and panicked like she'd been hit with an icy jet from a hydrant. She was taken by surprise, and her body responded badly. She surfaced with an emptiness in her eyes.

Closing off from Jay's sarcasm, Ash let the flower float from her, along with her rubber thongs. The bird of paradise stalk floated face down, without rescue. Jay realised Ash was hurt and moved towards her in the water. She seemed to have lost all her energy as she stood limply, fighting back the tears and then sudden rage, which she didn't know how to express.

'I haven't been in the water since—,' she gasped. 'I've been waiting for the time to be right... not yet, it's not yet.'

Jay embraced Ash, but something felt cold about him this time. He rolled his eyes as she confided in him. Empathy didn't come naturally to Jay. He released his embrace and climbed out of the pool, leaving Ash to collect her floating thongs, but not the flower.

Somebody was calling out, 'Ya missed the early ya kook!' then a lean figure appeared, balancing on the threshold of the back door. 'Jay? Wanna come out now? It's the sweetest offshore.'

It was Skinny. He was the most prolific surfer in the house, and almost always in the water. When he wasn't in the water, he was eating something, anything. He really was skinny, with rough short hair that looked like it'd been cut with a blunt knife. He had big teeth and a small strained smile. He reminded Ash of an otter or a rabbit. He seemed kind the way he acknowledged her with a nod. *Maybe more of a rabbit,* she thought.

'Come watch us?' Jay turned to Ash, outrageously ignoring what had just taken place.

Ash didn't feel like answering Jay and climbed out of the pool with effort. She stripped down to her bikini and hung her dress to dry over a faded deck chair. Skinny was staring at Ash while waiting for Jay's answer.

'Oy!' Jay territorially barked at Skinny. 'Wait out the front. I'll go up and get my board,' Jay commanded.

'Hey Ash, I'm sorry. It was just a little fun to get the day going. You had your bikini under your dress, and I thought you'd be okay... or else I wouldn't have done that to ya. Sorry, babe.'

Ash was distracted as she slid on her wet thongs. Jay came up behind Ash, wrapping her in a large beach towel and kissed her on the back of the neck.

'You look beautiful when you're wet,' he whispered. And with that, she forgave him, letting it all go.

Jay left Ash poolside to get his surfboard. He crossed paths with Oli on the staircase, who was bounding down in a way that you'd be expecting a frazzled Mother to cry out *Stop!* Oli had remembered something and froze in his tracks.

'Ya Dad called lookin for ya. Sounded like he was in a payphone ay... coughin' heaps.'
'The fuck I care,' Jay snapped.
'Sure man, whatever, he's ya Dad dude.'
'Yeah, so what?'
Oli shrugged at his bitter reaction and glanced at Jay's board. 'Hang on! I'm coming out.'

Ash passed by the kitchen and stopped to look at the photos on the fridge. There was an old newspaper clipping with Jay, and a guy wearing a surfing rashie covered in logos, complete with a lei around his neck. The inscription underneath said '*Troy 'Tora' Jones, with his young cousin Jay Knight, after successfully competing Oahu, Hawaii. 1987.*'

Jay entered the kitchen. 'Okay! Let's get going,' he sputtered, in an outburst to distract Ash from the picture.

'This is you? Your hair is so long. Is that Tora?'

'Oh yeah ... ages ago. C'mon. Yeah... the waves are waiting,' Jay breathlessly urged.

Jay took Ash's hand and led her outside where Oli and Skinny were waiting impatiently with their sticks, in the middle of the road.

The crew marched to the sea, not prepared to miss another moment of perfection. Finally, back at the lapping and frothing shore, their hungry eyes scanned the waves before they strapped on their leg ropes. To Jay, this felt like home. Ash watched the three boys run into the sea together.

Racer was already out the back. Jay paddled to his side.

'Nice catch,' Racer greeted Jay.

'Yep! I saw yours. Dude!' Jay thought Emma was a mess of a girl, and not worth the time of day.

'Mate, she passed out on me,' Racer concurred with a deadpan expression that was fixed to the horizon.

'Lucky break! She was hanging off Oli at the club early on. Man, you're a glutton for punishment,' Jay laughed at Racer's tragic comedy. This seemed to be a recurring theme lately.

As she lay waiting on the dry sifted sand, Ash watched her delicate hand eclipse the sun through red eyelids. She hoped to block the fireball just for a moment, to stop a beating headache from fully taking hold.

Eventually the surfers returned to her and Ash hazily stood to greet them. Momentarily she went unnoticed, so she stayed alone with her sunlit headache.

'Did you see the face of that last one? Broadies' had the best waves all week,' Jay gushed.

'Yeah, man. Can't get enough. I'm gonna finish shaping that new gun ay? I'm making the rails a bit thinner, and I'm fixin the channels,' Racer explained.

Oli chirped in, 'I wanna be the first one testing that swallow tail ya got in the shaping bay. When's it gonna be ready?'

Ash was quietly smiling, watching them speak their own rare language. She was amused that she didn't understand anything at all. The new girl.

Back at La Quinta, on that couch, all the guys, and Ash were sinking into its lumpy brown velvet while mesmerised by the television. Jay was flicking through the four channels. Channel 7: Donald Trump pornographically guffawed on a Baroque golden bed, dressed in a white bathrobe. Channel 9: The Price is Right with a hysterical woman running towards a new beige armchair, Channel 10: Oprah talking to some guy in a suit holding a chimpanzee, also in a suit; and the best choice of all, ABC 2: Rage, with a satisfying blast from the past, the Cindy Lauper *Time after Time* music video.

It struck Ash to see Cindy curled in her silver caravan, with her plastic dog, missing her Mother and watching television in the woods before deciding to pack her things and go, leaving her boyfriend behind. Cindy was miming the dialogue of an old film that Ash didn't recognise, but she did recognise the vase brimming with birds of paradise, front and centre of the scene. Twice in a morning Ash was shaken by symbols of Edie, as if her twin was reaching out to her. Ash didn't believe too much in signs, but Edie did. *It'd be just her style.*

Skinny noisily finished pulling a cone from his Orchy bottle, which saved Ash from bursting into tears of nostalgia and regret.

'Ahhh. I'm so hungry I could eat the crack of dawn,' Skinny murmured, then coughed.

Oli, Jay and Racer fell into exploding fits of laughter. Ash, much less amused, looked forward to going to her new job at Cult Kitchen. Her ticket to a brand new life.

'It's time to go to Old Man Chow's. Munchies!' Jay declared.

The guys lifted from the clutches of the brown couch and jackknifed themselves toward the front door. Jay grabbed a handful of coins which were scattered on the coffee table and let them clink into his board shorts pocket. Ash had to admit, it was easy to get these guys out of the house, they went empty handed. No shirts, no shoes, no keys, no money. Just their waxy hair, lazy grins and sculpted frames were enough to open most of the worthwhile doors in the neighbourhood.

'C'mon baby, I know you gotta work soon. Let's go!' Jay was trying to get Ash to stand up before the others lost momentum.

1'Yeah, I should get there early I guess. I'll walk with you then go straight to the cafe.'

Ash lifted herself and grabbed her bag. She was all set to leave that morning and that house behind.

⌒

Old Man Chow appeared to be a stern, middle-aged Chinese grocery store owner. He looked ever tidy with his balding head neatly combed, a constant grey cardigan and a highly buttoned powder blue shirt. His pursed lips were a sign of his patience, or perhaps a ticking time bomb, which could soon let out a yell to evacuate his store. Upon further analysis, Ash realised Old Man Chow was much more benevolent than stern, as his eyes followed Skinny zooming up and down the grocery store aisles on a pushie he had borrowed from outside. Old Man Chow's lips did not move. Nor his face. Just his piercing stare that was magnetised to the young man tearing up his serenity.

Ash and Jay were at the checkout. Oblivious to the unsettling scene, Jay counted out his coins for the two packs of Maggi 2 Minute noodles. He was being purposefully slow with his small change, as if that was going to even make a dent on Old Man Chows inner fury.

'Forty-seven… forty-eight! Haha! We have it!' Jay proudly reported.

He motioned to high-five Ash, and she responded with mild confusion. Ash quickly turned to see Skinny flying past on his new pint sized BMX up the aisle and out the entryway, drinking from an enormous orange juice carton.

'I need'a dollar for this, couldn't wait.' Skinny's words zoomed by just before the juice started to gush down his pelican throat.

'Sorry mate, don't have it!' Jay yelled without turning to see Skinny.

Old Man Chow glared at Jay and Ash harder, as if that was even possible. With this, Oli and Racer started skateboarding in the store on their new found wheels. It was humorous and terrorising at the same time. These guys could turn on all the charms of a homegrown three ring circus, and it was hard to tell if it was pure fun or simply criminal.

'Ahhh... a dollar? Yes, just give me a second... I think I have it.'

Ash couldn't take much more and was surrendering to her embarrassment. She fished around in her bag and found a dollar note for the simmering cashier. She placed it on the bench quickly and apologetically.

'Ok. I think you go now, yes, yes. Goodbye, good-bye,' Old Man Chow spat with a dismissing wave.

'Goodbye, goodbye, goodbye,' Jay childishly mimicked.

Ash blushed and took Jay by the hand to accelerate their welcomed departure. Jay was now laughing hysterically while holding Ash's hand and crossing the threshold, back out onto the pavement. Finally, Ash lit up and started to see the humour, from the safety of outside. The four guys together were indeed a pretty funny sight. Their laughter was infectious. To close off the comedy act, as if an encore was necessary, Jay ran a short distance and did a flip on the sidewalk.

'Right. Okay. Step aside,' Ash confidently ordered.

Ash put her bag on the ground, took a few exaggerated steps backward and stood on her toes. She skipped ahead, and in perfect form, did a forward flip that would make all the boys cry.

The boys were stunned by Ash's manoeuvre and soon started laughing even more as Oli and Skinny were quick to get started on doing cartwheels along the store fronts. Within ten seconds they were falling everywhere. The fun just as quickly ended when Skinny ungracefully crashed into a cafe table, knocking it and its spent cappuccinos and muffins flying.

'Oh God! This is Cult Kitchen! This is where my new job is,' Ash gulped as her face flushed.

Sam marched out of the cafe and looked at the scene and then looked to Ash who started to laugh uncontrollably.

'Well, maybe not anymore baby,' Jay summarised.

Now what? She slowly blinked in the wake of realising all was lost.

CHAPTER EIGHT

November Rain

The birdless sky canopied another black November morning, not that it meant anything. The rain fell all it could before daylight came and overhead would soon become a luminous grey. It was the ninth day of rain, and the swimming pool looked like an overfilled punch-bowl, with swirling frangipanis that took on the tones of over ripened fruit. The roof gutters had tapped their resentment rhythmically through the night like a ticking clock that goes unheard, until you don't want to.

Ash woke like a shot. A thought rang through the darkness louder than a fired gun. The house remained silent. It was only her, with her screaming thoughts, nobody else was to hear. *I want to leave him!* Her mind wailed. It had been nine weeks since she first woke in that single bed. More precisely, nine weeks had passed since Ash had taken refuge under the forever broken wing of La Quinta.

Ash lay sleepy eyed in Jay's tenacious grip, in his crooked bedroom, with her thighs pressed in between the cool fractured wall and his warm, blonde legs. Her hair fell mostly across her face in threads, but she didn't move a muscle, in case he stirred. There was no swell, and the house was still sleeping. *Was it because of the low-pressure system… or the high-pressure system? Or El Niño? Oh, whatever. Oh God! Why can't there be good surf?* Ash was lapsing into inconsequential thoughts more frequently, as if that's where she would find solace and sanity.

Lately, every waking moment that Jay was sleeping was Ash's asylum. She was tired, and he was relentless with demands for her attention. *It's all my fault,* she recited as she let the weeks tumble, falling deeper into the crevices of the house and its rituals. She was one of them now, but would never utter it aloud. Running with the pack, with no tomorrow, and seemingly invisible to the outside world, was her new reality. Surviving Jay's needs was Ash's initiation, and the truth was, she had nowhere else to be. Nowhere to go. She was broke, and if not for the determined grip of this man, she'd be alone. Being alone was not an option, not anymore. A dependency had crept upon them. Ash spent her days in Jay's routine and was succumbing to his insecurities. The chilling clarity washed over her as she lay in the darkness. She just couldn't leave. Maybe someday. When the coast was clear and the cage wide open.

Ash drifted into reflection of a golden afternoon that was more than a week before. She was giving a gymnastics lesson to Oli and Skinny on the front lawn, under the spinning water of the sprinkler, with their distorted shadows theatrical in the dissolving sunset. Those boys were like somebody's little brothers, living in a dilapidated house where Mother never arrived. There was still the threat of *'Wait till your Father gets home!'*, but Tora, the patriarch, wasn't due back until late January. Ash knew she needed to be gone by then. Probably impossible.

Ash wished last night was just a bad dream. Instead, it was a new low in her flea-bitten existence. She was working, finally booked for a Ravaged show. It was Ash's first swimwear parade in a month, and the money would have been a saviour. Everybody in the house had been beyond broke since Jay had the whole pack banned from the Social Security office two weeks before. He went in there and started yelling at the staff members, like a lunatic. He wanted his money, all of it, and he wanted it immediately. Two security guards waddled toward them with keys and flashlights jiggling, and they removed the whole gang. Expensive morning, that was. Ash wanted to go back and seek some kind of reconciliation, alone, but Jay wouldn't hear of it. So now porridge, pancakes and noodles were the sum of their food intake; in-between days when the boys would run the gauntlet at Old Man Chow's minimart—stuffing boxes of jelly crystals and Cup-a-Soup into their threadbare pockets.

The night before, at Island Dreams, Ash should have realised her entrapment, then and there. Instead, it took the whole dark night for the situation to sink in, and she felt nothing but responsible. To her surprise, and to the savage cheering of the audience, Jay climbed up onto the stage and dragged Ash off by the arm. At first, Ash thought Jay was joking, but he was serious. Blinded by jealousy to see *his girl* on stage spinning in a vortex of pulsing blue light and tufts of glitter, he climbed up there, like a big cat, and ferociously took what was his—and nobody stopped him. A lover's quarrel, that's all.

He pulled Ash all the way to the dressing room, commanded that she cover herself as he stuffed her things into her bag. He snarled that she had thirty seconds to get out of the club. It was time for him to take her home. He tailed her all the way to the exit, breathing down her neck and still clutching her arm. They pushed through the backdoor, and out into the rain.

Zoe had brought Ash's skateboard from her place. After a two month wait, Ash was finally reunited with her beloved board that seemed to emanate with colourful joy and memories of home. She couldn't wait to ride it, and Jay knew it. As he stormed up the wet street, he snatched the board from Ash's embrace and threw it into an alleyway industrial bin—as punishment for embarrassing him. He demonstrated his heartless force, and she exposed the depths of her passivity.

Beach Road to Monaco Street was an arduous walk in the rain. Ash trailed, like a scolded puppy behind her master, bowing at his sharpened words. Jay now had the taste of blood, and Ash's confidence was battered.

She shouldn't have been dressed like that in front of all those men, he was right. She was *his girl* now. How dare she. She berated herself.

Ash could feel the liquorice bruise on her arm, still rough with glitter, and painful under her weight as it pressed the hard mattress. The ticking water droplets carried on until the encrusted fly screen dispassionately funnelled in the new day.

Birdsong twirled above the steep roof pitches of Monaco Street and Ash grew anxious. That angelic face, asleep beside hers, with the heart-shaped mouth, would open its sapphire eyes at any moment, leaving Ash in anticipation of what would come forth, passion or poison. She had no appetite for either. Jay's slow breath quickened and his arm wrapped around Ash tighter, like a python.

'Hey, baby, I'm thirsty. What ya got?' Jay murmured into the pillow.

She sat up and flattened her palm on the window under the drape. There was a pleasure in touching the smooth glass that often gave a cool welcome on contact. She was tired of the rain but knew she would wish for it again soon. She was not sure what to expect of the famously hot Queensland weather since she had heard ominous tales of fire and wrath from the gaping jaws of her stoned housemates. *'Beautiful one day, apocalyptic the next,'* the boys would squawk in unison. Ash took the opportunity to finally pull her hair back into order with a loose top knot that looked like an old ball of pink and gold yarn. She reached for one of Jay's tee shirts at the foot of the bed and was snapped back into position with a whip of his arm.

'I'm thirsty for you baby, where are ya going?'
'I was going to go make you some coffee,' she quietly assured him, hoping to get a free pass out of there.

Before she knew it, Jay had her pinned underneath him, with her slender wrists clasped by his determined hand. He was ready for her. It wasn't a discussion. After a moment, his warm mouth was exploring her elongated neck, as he pressed against her hips with his. As always, it only took a moment for Jay to overcome Ash, breaking her resistance. She gave way to his desires every time. It was just easier.

Now the room was awake, and Jay wanted a coffee after all. Ash wandered down the hall, her eyes following her pink toes along the embossed swirls of the aquamarine carpet, like an easily distracted child, then down the twist of the sweeping staircase. The house was silent, except for the sound of Moose yawning and scratching feverishly, from the front door matt where he preferred to sleep. *Such a good dog.* Ash stopped on the bottom step to take in what she saw.

It was her, the girl with the green cellophane eyes. Sitting upright on the arm of the brown couch. Her auburn hair fell all around her shoulders in waves. It covered most of her torso, all the way down to her waist. Her hands rested on her naked thighs. Perfectly still, she watched Ash in the morning silence.

Beside the naked girl, was another girl, planted on a lumpy cushion. She was dressed in shorts and a boy's tee shirt, and was flicking through a copy of Surfing Life. Her legs were crossed, and her toes curled less than an inch away from the strange naked girl. She had cropped brown hair like a pixie, a button nose and her olive skin was sprinkled with chestnut freckles. She reminded Ash of a handsome teenage boy with long eyelashes and racehorse legs. Ash figured she must have come home with one of the guys last night—who knew? There was always a new chick.

'Hey there,' the boyish chick said and immediately went back to her magazine.

Ash returned a smile, but nothing more. The room felt askew. The emptiness was again filled when the naked girl spoke.

'I am the Other One,' the words dripped from her mouth so softly, they floated to Ash in an echo across the sparse loungeroom.

Ash felt the rush of a cold chill run up her arms, leaving a trail of goosebumps. The naked girl blinked heavily, as if underwater, like a siren.

'I'm Ash,' awkwardly and too late, Ash half raised a hand in greeting and felt perhaps more naked than the auburn haired girl.

Ash could have heard a pin drop in the seconds that followed. Nothing was happening. The naked girl continued to stare at Ash, studying her. Ash could do nothing but look away and busy herself with her need to go into the kitchen. *The other what?* Ash wondered as she finally left the staircase. Trying to normalise the scene, she raised her hand again.

'See you later,' Ash said with little effort.

The boyish girl was interrupted by Ash walking by and glanced up from her magazine briefly. It surprised Ash that she had no qualms about sitting and inch away from the naked one. *Geez, so much for personal space,* Ash was critical. She carried on toward the kitchen.

Ash took her time making the coffee in the ageing Laminex kitchen that was wall to wall orange. It was so out of style, it was almost chic. Sure, there were many elements rotten and broken, but still, it had its charm as the gracefully aged entertainers' kitchen. Its archway servery and two-way cocktail cabinets were set high above the central island, and hooks for pots and pans swung overhead the six-burner stove. *Whoever built La Quinta, really loved their food,* Ash appreciated as she waited for the kettle to sing.

As she stepped out of the kitchen carrying the coffees, Ash hesitated. She wasn't sure if she wanted to have another bizarre exchange with 'The Other One' and the boyish girl, and was relieved that the strange one was no longer on the couch. She was nowhere to be seen.

The boyish girl hadn't moved and continued reading, this time without acknowledging Ash as she passed by.

Jay was out of bed and hastily embraced Ash when she returned. She balanced the hot drinks expertly and looked over his shoulder with her eyes glazed as she blurred her view out the window that was now blasting with sunshine. Jay placed his coffee on one of the shelves in the built-in wardrobe and lifted his almost empty watering can. The built-in wardrobe in their bedroom was not for clothes. It was a nursery.

Jay had created the perfect set up. The wardrobe had sliding wooden doors that ran the width of the bedroom. The interior hanging area was lined with aluminium foil and a hot lamp system that fit plants up to a few feet high. The smaller shelves were for seedlings and drying. Jay had propagated his very own marijuana crop, right under Tora's nose. Ash wondered if all the boys had wardrobes like this in the house since they seemed to have an endless supply of weed. The idea that it was illegal, and they could get in trouble with the cops, didn't even cross her mind. Ash had until now, spent zero time thinking about drugs and the law. It just hadn't been in her sphere.

Ash sipped her coffee and watched Jay busy himself with his money trees before remembering that she too, had a garden to tend. Ash took advantage of Jay's distraction of tending to his precious crop. She crossed the hall with a glass of water left from the night before and delicately trickled it down the gnarled, tiny trunk of the bonsai tree in Tora's bedroom. Feeding the hungry undergrowth that was delightfully reaching for the sun rays, had become a ritual. Ash was beginning to learn the rhythm of the tree, it's ebb and flow, and the energy it gave the room. Ash had realised the bonsai was an Oak, and it made her feel intrinsically linked to Edie and her final resting place, a million miles away.

The stillness of the house and of Jay's mood was pleasant for now, and Ash felt like spending time on making things a bit more liveable. She decided to fix something that usually ruined her day, and made her feel like she was living like a cockroach. She wanted to tackle the bathroom cleaning. It looked like it had not been done for years. It was diabolical. Ash felt compelled to treat it as a manageable problem and fix it herself. There was part of her that refused to admit that she wanted to clean it for Jay and the boys. She was trying not to picture herself as Cinderella or even worse, Snow White. At least Cinderella escaped that house with a handsome prince and new shoes, without too much of a wait. Snow White had a rougher ride, she always felt, with that poisonous apple and all. It was not a far stretch for her to imagine Jay as the Evil Queen or the Wicked Stepmother or any similar archetype on most days, and those boys that came and went, full of trouble and strife, like the Seven Dwarves, rather than the Ugly Sisters.

Ash cleaned the filthy bathroom. She scrubbed the tea cup bath of it's swirling grime, then the whole room, floor to ceiling, as best she could. As a last task, and by now exhausted, she cleaned the cracked mirror, taking a moment to study her sorry reflection. The bathroom was now brighter, but she was unable to find the satisfaction she expected on the other side. She sat on the little curry powder tiles and leaned against the tub. She scanned the haunted room imagining if the walls could speak and sensed their dourness.

It was Ash's responsibility to keep the house flush with toilet paper. Usually no problem, but without money, it was closer to a hunter-gatherer task. A few blocks away there was an old strip mall with public toilets out the back, complete with broken doors and a lax security system. Now was a good a time as any to go up there and claim her weekly haul. She took an empty shopping bag and wandered west along Monaco Street, towards the old shops.

The building looked like an old egg carton made with undercooked blonde bricks and a wide-brimmed roof that pushed the walls into the earth. As an architect's daughter, Ash was not one to comment if it was ugly or not, but she did see the design effort as something less than remarkable, in her opinion. The building, paralleled with a confused landscape of cactus, appeared displaced among the tropical heirloom cultivars and low stone walls that lined the street. Set back on large waterfront blocks were bungalows, one more quirky than the next. Their gardens were inhabited by white swans of cut car tyres, or handmade concrete borders pressed chaotically with local seashells that looked like squabbling children had decorated a mud cake.

As a resident of La Quinta, Ash was street wise and approached the toilet block with caution. She entered with her ears first, and would go to the trouble of not breathing so she could listen hard. The coast was clear, it always was. But today, something different, a shoe box was oddly left in the centre of the floor. It was moving ever so slightly, and Ash approached it warily before opening it. Her heart was racing, expecting there might be a rat that had found itself stuck.

At first glance, it just seemed dark inside, then she saw a little pink mouth stretching wide in yearning. The tiniest kitten was tucked in the corner, peering up to the light. Green eyes like marbles were staring back at Ash, and that little mouth was filled with baby white fangs that framed inaudible cries. Its ebony powder puff paws recoiled, demanding to be scooped up by Ash's tender hands. She immediately rolled a pouch into her tee shirt and swaddled the weightless fluff ball for the walk home.

CHAPTER NINE

This Year's Girl

The rain was constant over Tokyo, dragging the city colours down the forlorn window panes, and finally infusing puddles on the inky streets below. It looked so beautiful through the sheer drapes as the eclectic glow of light whispered into the room. Asuka wished she could hear the rain's melancholy as she waited for Tora on the 22nd floor. The hotel room was finished with salmon pink and straight lines of mahogany, giving way to the sea mist green carpet that was doing its best to look awake, after all these years.

Asuka took the little cardboard disk off a drinking glass in the dim marble bathroom and poured herself some gin. Tonight she felt thirsty and nervous. It had been more than three months since she had seen Tora, and so much had happened. She had much to tell, much to confess.

Her hair was the blackest of black, with bangs that kissed her eyelashes with every gentle blink. Her gothic skin was brightly contrasted against her black leather dress, which corseted her pounding heart and decadently pinched waist. Moments earlier, Asuka had changed her lip colour from Vendetta Red to Cherry Blossom Pink, hoping to change the tone of the reunion to something more nostalgic, only to change her mind again. It would be the Vendetta Red that Tora tastes tonight, she had decided for him.

Asuka was pure of heart, yet a selfish lover. She was trapped in the throes of a demanding career in Osaka working for a cosmetics company and feared she had left it all too late. At thirty-one, she had become insatiable, and most recently, her need to feel sexually desired had overwhelmed her life. She was a beautiful woman, and had made a career of it, travelling the world as a fashion model. Untouchable by all—except for Tora. But that was years ago.

Her affair with Tora had been erratic and passionate, encased with a sense of tragedy that drifted through their memories like French perfume. She adored him when she was with him. He found her impossible to hold down, and felt lucky to have had her at all. He called her his Koi.

In the early years, he wanted her to move to Australia with him. This idea was far from Asuka's ambitions, and she routinely and flatly refused his proposals. Tora carried on loving her. Following her. Meeting her whenever she made herself available, from one hotel room to the next, all over Japan. He made her feel like a woman, which Asuka thought sounded like a cliché, except it was true. His hands would bridge her tiny waist, and she would feel engulfed by passion when he kissed her with all his love. He overwhelmed her physically, and she relished feeling like a naked porcelain doll in his clutches. He was dominant when she needed to feel fragile. *Like a woman should,* she believed. Her power over him had been immense, ever since that first time they met in a photographic studio. He had just won his first surfing title, and she her first Vogue spread.

Seven long years later, and here they stood face to face in the doorway of room $N^{\underline{o}}$ 2207 of the downtown Tokyo Marriott. Tora wondered why her lips were such an ominous red. He wasn't sure if he could kiss them. Asuka fell into his gaze immediately and found all she could do was reach out her hand and softly touch his hip. He looked different tonight, tired. Her nervousness echoed.

'Asuka,' no sound came. 'Hello, my Koi,' he finally said aloud.

She found herself silent and returned a Japanese smile. He knew then he could not kiss her and that she was no longer his. Her hand dropped from his waist, and he closed the door behind him.

'It's after midnight. Are you alright?'
'I was lonely, I needed to see you before I leave,'

her eyes changed colour.

'I thought you were here all week?' Tora was disappointed.

'I have to fly to Paris in the morning. I'm leaving Japan. I'll be gone long time.'

Tora crossed the room, entranced by the glow of the window and the refraction his impaired vision gifted him in this moment. The rain systematically swirled the colours left to right, up and down. He always felt confused when he was with her. Tora never understood love, if that's what it was, or wasn't. When she looked at him, with those teary black eyes, his heart would be stabbed with a feeling of loss. That feeling of loss was all he knew now when it came to women. He reached out to touch the window, wishing he could be back out there in the rain. He found he often wanted to turn back time. This was an unsettling idea for a man that used to live without regrets.

'Before I go, I wanted to tell you something...everything,' she sighed.

Tora turned to Asuka and stepped closer to her. He gently cupped her face in his hands. His tanned skin was like caramel against her creamy cheeks. She looked through her black fringe, her red lips parted involuntarily, as she breathed in his salty scent. Now all she wanted was him to kiss her the way he always did. She put her pale hands over his, urging him to move in closer, but it was futile.

'Don't tell me everything. I know Asuka, I know,' he continued to hold a whisper, not to disturb the crystalline atmosphere. 'I was never enough. You needed more. You wanted everything. One man will never be enough for a girl like you.'

Asuka's eyes welled. It was as if he wrote her. He knew it all, as he always did. Tora's intensity and indifference to her confessions made her blood run hot. She stepped back from him and assuredly reached for the zipper of her dress. With absolute conviction, Tora didn't react. Asuka's black leather dress fell heavily on the sea mist carpet, along with her restraint. She stood before him almost naked, exposed and available. She then moved to lay on her back, on the bed, under Tora's wooden gaze. It only took a second for her to feel her isolation before she started to weep. Asuka had no more of a persuasive invitation for Tora. With every second that he didn't submit, she cried more deeply. Everything had surged within her, and her love for him started to pour out in waves. She now wanted him to commune with her for just one more night, but he was lost.

'Please Tora. Why don't you hold me?' Asuka whimpered.

Their rapport had turned from romantic to erotic years before, and Tora was left to see her body panting and wanting, blindfolded by her own tears for the last time. He approached the bed and put his hands on her legs and dropped to his knees. He stared at the floor for some time, as he felt her trembling under his cool grasp.

He breathed in her familiar *honey cake* scent and looked up to see the glare of her milky thighs, all the way to her glittering silver g-string. He traced the line of her body with his hands until they were on her bent knees, he pushed them further apart, slowly, like a forbidden gateway. He slid one hand along the inside of her thigh and gently guided the silver thread of her underwear aside. He kissed her leg and then licked her lavishly, only once, before rising to his feet.

'I loved you, Asuka. You taught me many things about the heart. You spoke to me in so many ways. You were like a wild animal to me, one I could never catch... and you still elude me. I remember when we met, you told me I could never possess you because your name meant tomorrow, and tomorrow never came.'

Tora paused and created distance between them. 'Do you remember the first place I kissed you?'

'My pussy,' Asuka elegantly whispered with her wet eyes tightly closed.

Tora moved towards the door and half opened it. 'I'll miss you,' he professed.

The door closed, and they were both freed.

CHAPTER TEN

I Wanna Be Sedated

The long day was finally caving in. The sky looked like an exhausted candle, as the obstinate flame licked the horizon. Ash watched the day's death through the bedroom window. She had spent countless hours in that room by now, being the last half of January. She could hear the tin roof crackle and ping in the heat outside.

Jay had pulled the fly screen all the way off the frame so he could climb out onto the roof at any given moment. The rooftop had become somewhat of a private balcony, extending the bedroom onto the corrugated platform. By mid-morning, La Quinta's burnt orange top usually felt like it might buckle with heat exhaustion. Jay would sit with his legs dangling over the gutter, flicking cigarette butts down into the jungled palm grove. He smoked now. Ever since that Christmas party on Seagull Ave.

Jay did a lot of things now that Ash struggled with. She had found, in a Pavlovian manner, that if she just stayed in that bedroom, on that little bed, keeping quiet, not too much would go wrong. It's not that his temper was too short, perhaps it was that Ash did too many things wrong that upset the balance of the relationship. Ash would contemplate how Jay could be so strong and yet so delicate all at once. She wanted to try harder to keep the waters calm for him. He was obviously going through something deeply internal, given the smoking and short fuse.

Stretched out on the bed beneath the window, with Ninja her black kitten curled on her legs, was not a terrible place to be. If she could just stay quietly there, not rock the boat, the day would end gracefully. Jay was out for his afternoon surf and was due back anytime. Then they would cook dinner, eat it on their bed together, or even out on the roof as the night cooled.

It had been ages since Ash had the peace of mind to draw. It was her true passion and she was once prolific—she'd once hoped to make it her life. Drawing with moments of overlapping poetry would bring richness to her creative expression and would help extract her fears and desires. In the old world, she would sit out in Henry's garden under the weeping willow that was all the way down the back, and daydream with her mind wide open, like a sunflower. Edie was the real writer though, so Ash never pursued it with any honesty.

Ash had kept a Tupperware container tucked under the bed. It was full of her drawings and poetry, as well as polaroids, mostly of her and Edie. It was central to her 'house fire' stash that she had initially packed before leaving Black Ridge. Ash spread the contents out onto the bed and studied what she had with admiration. She decided to stick a few of her best photos and drawings onto the bedroom wall.

La Quinta shuddered when the front door slammed, and Ash's smile fell. Jay's pounding footsteps drew near. There he was, with savage red eyes glowering and his salty chest heaving, as his shoulders rose. His hair clung to him like a wet stole. He didn't speak for some time, and Ash knew that her next move had to be well measured. If she asked him if he was okay or what was wrong too soon, he would explode in a fury. If she left it too long, there would be a cascade of consequences. Ash set the kitten aside and sat up more attentively to face him as he sat on the edge of the bed with his head in his hands. She reached out to touch him, and he was quick to snap back, flicking her hand away as if it were a wasp. Confused, as always, Ash withdrew.

'Broke my fuckin' board! That fuckin' gook dropped in on me. I'm gonna smash'im,' so loudly and deeply, he frightened her.
'Who baby? Where's the board? Maybe I can find a way to get if fixed.'

Wrong answer. Jay stood up from the bed roughly, pushing it hard against the wall and clenching his fists white. Eventually he turned to Ash. He came in close over her with a burning stare and lowered his face to hers. She was not sure what to do next. How was she meant to react? What was her facial expression supposed to be? *Stay blank. Don't move,* she voicelessly guided herself.

'It was fuckin' Johnny. And No! Ya can't fix it. What? Huh? How you gonna do that?' he carried on poking a finger at her temple. 'Are ya dumb?'

He turned again to leave the room, but stopped and punched the wall beside the door with his right hand, leaving an impression, another fracture, in Ash's eggshell universe. Jay dropped his chin and turned back to Ash for another round. He approached the bed and with one swoop, collected and scrunched several of her drawings that were on the bed infront of her. As a last word, he took the picture of her and Edie she had just stuck to the wall and flicked it onto the floor.

'No hangin fuckin' photos... so fuckin' selfish. I'm goin out. You're such a bitch Ash. Never wanting to help me when I really need it. You don't give a fuck about me or anybody else. No wonder your Mother can't stand the sight of you,' Jay grabbed a tee shirt from a fresh pile Ash had washed earlier that day. 'I don't know when I'll bother coming back... but don't you fuckin' leave this room. You hear me?'

He raised his hand to Ash's cheek and then stopped before hitting her. He finally exited the house with another shuddering slam. Ash was grateful that he didn't hit her. He hardly ever hit her.

ⱷ

The Playroom was pumping harder than usual for a Tuesday. The Ramones were in town, and this was the first gig Jay had been to in weeks. There'd been a buzz on the street about it for ages. He couldn't get there soon enough and hitched a ride straight up the highway from Surfers with a bunch of kooks. It was always a challenge to get into the club before dark since Jay was banned for life last summer, but when he was wired like this, he found solutions and backdoors. Jay had so much angst to release that the mosh pit alone wasn't going to cut it. There were no big waves to pound him, that angry sea was nowhere, so he sought the next best thing. He was looking for Maddie. He wanted to fuck, hard, that's all. Maddie was his girl for that, and damn, he loved that ripe ass.

Maddie loved Jay. She first met him at La Quinta almost two years before, when the boys threw a pool party on New Year's Eve. She went there with China and some guys from Palmy. The party was outrageous, and predictably, the cops came well before midnight after one of the guys had almost drowned (and another lost an eye) when he hit his head on the edge of the pool while taking a running leap onto a surfboard. Maddie never really got to speak to Jay that night, not because of the mayhem, but because he was with his girl, Nebraska Parkes.

Jay called her Nina, and she was American. She had a coven of qualities and was some kind of exchange student that never left. That wasn't her intention. She was so beautiful that nobody ever spoke to her. She was hard to look at. She was a trap because you couldn't look away. And that's just what the girls were saying, let alone those boys in the den with them. Jay may have been a wolf, but Nebraska, clever, slender, quick and venturous, was a fox. Nebraska had Jay under her thumb. Jay wanted her to have his babies and get married, but Nebraska was too wild. She was with Jay ten months, living with the pack, and was overdue to return across the Pacific to her home in Santa Rosa. *The Queen of Monaco Street* they used to call her, that summer. She seemed above everything, and with a green-eyed glance, Jay would drop to his knees for her.

One night the lovebirds had a big fight outside on the street. It tuned out that Jay wanted Nebraska to take morphine that he'd stolen from his Dad, and she refused. Things escalated, and he struck her, leaving a bruise on her face. Nobody could believe Jay would do that to his Queen. She ran to the sea, and he followed her. They were gone the longest time, on the beach, in the rain, and then they came back, and he was holding her chilled pale hand lovingly.

All of this was just before Jay's eighteenth birthday, which was the night Nebraska left the party and went surfing with Jay, along with a bottle of tequila. She never returned. Jay came home alone after a drunken search, hysterical. Tora went out looking for Nebraska and was gone hours before he raised the alarm. Her body couldn't be found.

After that night, Jay stayed in his bedroom for almost two months. When he finally came out, he didn't speak, he just mumbled Henry Rollins lyrics to himself, interspersed with tortured yells. He surfed until dark, searching for her, and his own soul, everyone thought.

Maddie was voluptuous. She was also blonde, which helped her cause. Her cause being, she was on a hedonistic pursuit. All those boys wanting to pound her made her feel pretty, there was no other way for her to ever feel pretty surrounded by surfer chicks and glamour models—this was the Gold Coast after all. Beauty was the currency habitually traded, above board and without remorse. She worked with what she had, which included a little freckle above her lip, like a movie star, and brown eyes that gave nothing too much away (although she wished they were blue). She had a tendency to not wear underwear and advertised it to any skeg that may have wondered what was up that micro skirt of hers. All the girls called her the *Town Bike*. It was hard to find a guy who hadn't ridden her. Maddie had an infectious laugh and could hold her drink, especially bourbon. Most boys couldn't say no to Maddie, and Maddie never said no to Jay. To her, he was a dream, way out of her league, but when he wanted her, she felt rich beyond any currency.

It was almost midnight and Ash had resigned to waiting up for Jay, right there in the bedroom like he told her to. She figured it was worth it. She didn't want to fight anymore. Hunger wasn't going to take over, and it wasn't worth going to the kitchen anyway. There wasn't much left to eat, and the last time Ash opened the oven a rat ran out, much to the hysteria of Oli and Skinny. They chased it, scampering up the halls like blind dogs, they really were useless hunters. The rat still lurked in the house, somewhere, and those boys were still talking about it.

Out on the roof, there was an elegant stillness as Ash looked to the billion-year-old stars. '*You are made of stardust,*' Henry used to always remind his twin daughters, with every tear and scratched knee, sealed with an Eskimo kiss. He would light their way with his fables of old. He claimed they were classic old tales, but the twins knew he was making up stories on the fly, as he fumbled through fatherhood under Joan's ever-present distance.

Ash crouched like a bird on the edge of the roof. She stared into the palm grove, with its silhouette arching towards her, black as a cloud of bats. It made a perfect backdrop for the sparklers she found earlier that day in her *firebox*. She lit the first one and felt satisfied as the flame took hold and ignited with a flash. She watched the mesmerising drag of colour the fiery sparks left across the Milky Way, as she cupped the galaxy in her hand. She found herself smiling at the spectacle of light she had created. The sparkles, and the rest of the universe, reflected in her moist eyes as she sat meditatively and watched the remains burn down to a charred stalk. She was alone again, waiting for him.

Dawn arrived. A murder of crows moaned hungrily overhead, and Jay looked like a cadaver lying covered in dried blood on a Chevron Island garden bed, but he wasn't dead. He was without his shirt and shoes, sprawled and still drunk. Jay had been in a dog fight, that's for sure. His Volleys were on the other side of enormous iron gates that sealed the circular driveway of a sleeping mansion. His shirt was hanging like a ripped flag of surrender from the manicured pandanus across the cul-de-sac. There were elliptical black skid marks on the street, and it looked like a rain of broken glass had showered the somnolent bitumen.

Jay was in the wrong neighbourhood. His blood-encrusted face began to animate as the dewy morning kissed his cheek. The menacing sound of irrigation spikes reaching up for their attack filled his head, and Jay sat up before he was able to fully open his eyes. When he did, he knew he was lost. It didn't matter. He'd found Maddie and got his fix. He had done enough damage to make the night worthwhile.

CHAPTER ELEVEN

Introduce Yourself

It was Australia Day and Joan Smith was turning fifty. Although her twin girls had abandoned her in her forty-ninth year, she was coping. She had to. Otherwise there'd be nobody to look after their Father, Henry Smith. Well, that was what she had based her dignity on. Being the eternal carer for a man, in actual fact, perfectly capable. Joan had remained closed for most of her life and had seeped lapses of joy when she first fell in love, first became a Mother, and when she was awarded her Masters Degree in something too complicated to explain to her children. All the millions of moments in-between were nothing, never making a ripple in her inhospitable universe. To Ash, it was as if she was sitting in readiness to expire. She found it sad that some do not cherish each breath they take, and others are never allowed to even dream of their potential—pushed back into the earth before they can stand on their own two feet.

Ash wondered if her Mother missed her, or found any discomfort at all, in not knowing exactly where she was. Ash last tried to call home in September. There was no answer, there was never an answer. Maybe they'd gone away somewhere. Maybe they moved. Maybe Joan had finally expired. Nothing really mattered now, Edie was gone. Ash was without a family.

The kitchen's Sunnyboy orange bench tops were more than Ash could bear in her pitiful state. It was another long night of revelling at La Quinta, and Ash still hadn't slept, not since yesterday, or maybe the day before. Her head was buzzing with tiredness and a little vodka. Her eyes were sticky, and she wasn't sure if she wanted to see anymore, anyway. The house was finally empty, back to bare bones, and the boys were tucked in their quarters. Ash stared at the phone that was fixed to the brash orange and lemon wallpaper, that looked like looped racing car tracks, in ten-foot-high repetition. There was something about that orange phone. It represented a beacon to Ash, a forbidden one, with its coiled cord perfectly underused and full of spring. It beckoned her to pick up the receiver and dial home, *just this once.*

Ash prized her heavy chest and one-tonne-head off the bench and found her posture. She inched forward to reach the phone and dialled. o—2—7—0—7—2—6—5—o. Heart racing. Ring... ring... ring.

'Hello.' Joan Smith formally enquired. 'Hello?'

Silence.

Ash realised she was unable to speak, and paralysed with emotion, her body had broken down. A silent outburst forced Ash's chin to fall as she tried to control her words, and she could no longer see through the distortion of tears.

Jay's hand came out of nowhere and crashed down on the receiver. The call was cut. Ash turned left to right in a panic, not sure whether to run, hide or freeze. She'd had a fright and her shoulders started to shake. Jay pulled her towards him assuredly, he held her face and kissed her forehead tenderly, before wiping a tear. Ash tried to pull away but was pacified by his embrace. He pulled her close and Ash's face became wrung with sorrow.

'What are ya doin Ash?' he whispered and squeezed her.

'It's my Mum's birthday today.'

'Don't worry about it. She never even called ya for Christmas,' he still spoke softly.

'She doesn't even know I'm here,' Ash muttered into Jay's smooth arm.

'Sure she does. We sent'er a card. Don't ya remember?' he was grasping at straws now. 'Come to bed, you're just tired and need a long rest,' he was close to convincing her to let go of home. 'You'll need to sleep before we go to Fisho's this arvo. Nirvana? Remember babe? We'll hitch down there and jump the fence,' he chortled, trying to lift her. 'You gotta be awake for that!'

It was early afternoon, and Ash felt physically refreshed after a few hours sleep under Jay's grip and the purring Ninja. She felt more robust now, but the heaviness of tears was still deep in her chest. There was an air of devastation at her foundation. Ash knew she was a victim of some sort, and honestly hoped she would survive Jay. Yes, it was questionable sometimes, when he really flew off the handle, but she felt she could survive this, all of this. She knew she would leave soon. She would get the courage to just stand up, pack her cotton shoulder bag and stride up Monaco Street, all alone, with nowhere to go and no money or help at all. She would be fine. *Gulp.*

Ash sat up in bed and studied her bare legs. They were bruised, but she couldn't remember how. Her skin was pale compared to the caramel suntan she had just a couple of months ago. Ash had made a habit of covering herself up during the past several weeks, as to not attract attention from other guys, especially passers by. If a guy even sideways glanced in her direction, Jay would threaten to punch them in the face, or worse, he would punch them in the face. He'd get a crazed look that turned his eyes violet, and almost transparent. He'd clench his fists and strike without hesitation, putting all his power behind his punch, from the ground and up through his body and out onto Loverboy's face. Jay was like some kind of machine when it came to expressing physical force. He was only nineteen, and at that age he knew too much about dishing out pain.

A few weeks before Jay had even screamed at an officer in a police car, accusing him of looking at his girl's legs, even though Ash was trailing behind in an oversized stolen tracksuit. If she could immerse completely into invisibility, that would be ideal. *More peaceful and far less dangerous for everybody,* she thought.

The next thing to go, now that her strong tender limbs were disguised under glaring white polyester, was her blonde tendrils of silken hair. Ash saw only a history of tales, ones of Edie and of being lost—she was lost in so many ways now. Her hair used to make her feel like it was part of her personal heritage and her bond with her twin. A sign of wellbeing and also the first thing newcomers would notice about her and Edie, since they made sure they kept their hair the same length, always. It was glorious once.

Ash found a big old pair of black sewing scissors in the shaping bay. Racer was handy like that, he always had the right tool for the job. Ash stood before her cracked amber reflection in the half-lit bathroom and measured a three-finger span below her shoulders. She grabbed a waist-length handful, and bluntly carved and chopped until that Golden Fleece of hers had dropped, followed by a well of silver tears.

Everybody was going to that Nirvana gig later and Jay was in high spirits. They'd sold heaps of weed for the long weekend and had a bit of cash. He was out the back with the boys drinking a slab of XXXX in the pool, since there was no surf. The ocean had been like a lake for the longest time. It felt like forever to Ash, she missed going down the beach, even if she had to watch Jay surf, it had become essential and somehow, cleansing. Ash knew she was in the process of transformation, maybe not in the right direction, but still, it seemed imperative that she changed, evolved somehow. Cutting her hair was an enormous step, all that pain and history was no longer hanging around her delicate neck. In a way it felt like a gesture of surrender to Ash. Acknowledging her circumstances and trusting that new experiences and love would emerge.

She was ready to take a few small liberties to help herself. She decided to put on her tangerine bikini and grab a towel—she was headed for the beach and would take a self prescribed essential swim. *I'll be quick, and Jay won't even notice,* Ash lied to herself, as she habitually did lately.

In the sea alone, Ash was swimming, for the first time in months, and given the lack of waves, and the long hot weekend, it was more like soup. Throngs of tourists in all shapes and sizes bobbed and rolled in the shallows with delight as their milky shoulders turned beetroot. Ash swam out deeper than the others, which was easy. She realised that she'd come a long way from not being able to go into the water at all, since Edie drowned that first Monday of July. It had been over six months now, and each day Ash had dragged herself through. The span of grief over time had been unimaginable, and previously never contemplated by Ash. She always assumed they would die together, and why not? They were born together. Was that so naive? There had been moments when Ash thought it only fair to their sister-hood, that she should die now too, but the flame inside would not grow dim enough for her to extinguish. Ash lived in the grip of sorrow, and perhaps it was guilt, but sometimes she dared not let the despair escape her for too long. A penance of sorts, leaving her to touch emotional extremities from one moment to the next.

She was way out now, in over her head, and far enough away from other beachgoers to take off her top and swim with a sense of freedom, which was to her, one of the most pleasurable things in life. Fully submerged and almost naked, enjoying the dappled sunlight that warmed the Pacific pond was healing. She swam further and further out, letting the slack tide pull her, drifting this way and that. *Days like this are one in a thousand,* Ash thought with a smile. The scorching heat was tamed by the blue wash of clear water. Fish were abound, and Ash could see the sandy bottom, combed by the constant motion of the sea as the earth inhaled and exhaled, assuredly and without a care.

Far beneath her, Ash saw something shiny as it caught the sun. She swallowed a lung full of summer air and pushed down to the ocean floor with her bikini top loose around her neck. Letting the salt sting her eyes, she retrieved the sparkling treasure. Clutching it, she returned to the surface to reclaim her breath. Ash studied it carefully as it rested, glistening in her wet palm, while her mermaid legs worked mechanically treading the water. Ash had found herself a Japanese fifty yen coin. The kind with a hole in the middle. She was charmed and attached the coin to her neck chain. With a toothy smile, acknowledging something fun and beguiling had actually happened to her, Ash put on her bikini top and swam back to the white-hot shore with vigour.

◦◦

Tora watched the barren marshland that held the bay, slide beneath him in a blur as the runway rippled and evaporated into a mirage. He was grateful to finally be on home turf and far from the blazing white snowcaps of Japan, where he had left his old thinking.

Johnny was waiting at the arrival gate, tapping a new beat on his black stovepipes and itching for a cigarette. He was intolerant of people that clustered as they wandered around the terminal like tumbleweeds, and found himself a corner of the waiting zone with a perfect vantage.

He never said it, of course, but he was a fish out of water on the Gold Coast without Tora. Johnny boyishly counted down Tora's return, mostly to reel in the end of a too-long summer.

Forever discreet with his affection, Johnny tried not to smile, and raised a slow hand, half-mast, when Tora appeared at the arrival gate. They strolled back to the car park as the urgency of the airport fell away. Small talk was resolved with silence as their stride struck the ground in effortless unison.

'How was the gig last night?' Tora interrupted the silent bond, more invigorated than tired after the long haul flight.

'I cut it short. Fucking drummers. I need a drum machine. An obedient Casio,' Johnny snapped and chased his remark with a grin.

'Yeah, you keep saying.'

'Remember that girl on the cover of SKTR magazine from last year? The skater girl with pink hair?'

'Ha! Yeah,' Tora reflected, of course, he remembered, he was obsessed with her picture and referred to her as *My Bride* to Johnny in jest, all last summer.

'Ha. I'm sure she was backstage at the club with the Ravaged chicks. The night you left and a couple of times since. Couldn't believe it when I saw her. The timing man.'

'You didn't give her your *look* did you?' Tora slapped his knee. 'You can't do that! You're a mean looking dude. She would've left town by now because of you. Thanks!'

'What look?' Johnny joked as Tora took time to assess his expression.

'Damn. *Tokidoki warau*. The lady killer,' Tora looked at Johnny who was trying to smile, which apparently didn't come naturally. It was more like a tight grimace that unhappily affected his whole face. He was a hilarious guy once you were attuned to the nuance of his humour.

The brown hardscape of the blurred highway edge pulled Tora back into his old worries. He tried not to imagine what waited for him at home. He'd spent the last months mentally preparing to clear out the house, and his life, but it was going to take work and unfortunately, displace a few of the younger ones, including Jay. Tora had reached a point of clarity and spent hours thinking, as well as discussing in fireside conferences with his Mother, Myrtle.

By the time the Beast rolled into the city limits, a new wave of optimism had washed in over Tora's woes. *She* was in town, that girl. He had a feeling he'd be able to find her, well he had decided he would. So he would.

_____

The lounge room lacked light although the front window was now smashed to smithereens. Its fragments and shards surrounded the armchair, outside on the uncut grass. The front yard had a new spectacle: a tattered armchair, the latest victim of Jay's flammable demeanour.

Jay's bruised and bleeding hands were clenched into fists. He released them and stretched his cold fingers before wiping his bloody hands on his tattooed chest. His slow hands moved up to his stone face, and he pulled back his hair, straining his scalp. His bloodshot eyes revealed to Ash, a sense of terror, like a bull ready to rush his opponent. He had reached new heights and felt unstoppable, and that's what terrified him more than anything.

'I love you,' Jay whispered to a trembling Ash, her hair still wet from the sea.

'I'm sorry... I was only swimming... baby.'

Jay firmly grabbed her chin with his bloodied hand. He forced eye contact, then gently put his palm on her cheek.

'If you ever leave this house without me again—'
'I'm sorry, yes,' she obeyed.

Jay walked away from the broken window into the darkened halls of the house. Ash, shaken, chose not to follow him as she usually would, and instead lightly stepped outside to the front yard. She felt out of her body as she wandered over the threshold. She was not physically hurt, but he had finally killed her—her lifeforce now depleted.

Tora and Johnny pulled up outside the house, and all of Tora's fears were realised. The long grass was home to broken bikes, skateboards, beer bottles and palm throngs. There was also, of course, the most recent addition—the armchair that had taken exit through the front window. The most obscure thing of all was the slight figure of a girl in a tangerine bikini, standing with slumped shoulders over the armchair, looking at it like a strange man's corpse.

'Fuck. Jay's been busy,' Tora was almost breathless with frustration.

Ash looked back to the street to see the mean-looking car resting at the curb. She stopped. Everything stopped.

Tora emerged from the passenger side and slammed the door before the car pulled away with a tenacious growl that stuck to the bitumen. He was tall and athletic with unkempt hair, just as she had remembered. Ash struggled to see his face in the blinding sunlight. It didn't matter, she defiantly looked toward the sun.

Tora stopped at the footpath and watched Ash for a moment. He noticed her fixed gaze and approached her slowly, stopping at her side. They both stared at the chair blankly. There were no words that belonged to that chair. Too much had already been said. The subject was mute. Ash turned to Tora, with anguished eyes, there was no hiding it, not anymore. Jay had toppled her once and for all. Her trembling fingers lifted and wiped the feint blood and tears from her face. Tora spoke first without looking at her, he couldn't. He felt ashamed.

'Why are you here? Go home.'
'I... I am... I can't.'

Tora finally turned to look at her face and could see the little girl within, scampering for corners to bow her narrow body into. *What had he done?* He knew at that moment, Jay was a killer.

Jay stepped out from the house's interior darkness and approached Tora tentatively to greet him.

'Hey. Tora. Ahhh... How was your trip?'
'Who's she? Is this gonna be the same as what you did to the *other one*?'

Jay had nothing to say. He clenched his triangle jaw and arched his back like a hyena when he found he was unable to look at Ash in Tora's presence. He knew all too well the simmering anger loaded in Tora's accusation. Now was not the moment for retaliation. Tora's glare locked onto Jay as he pushed past him to enter his home.

Ash felt her fear unfurl as she witnessed the exchange. Tora pushed Jay aside like a sulking child and stopped at the threshold. He turned to look at Ash, he saw those doll eyes, and it churned him. She looked familiar, and it hurt.

It was close to midnight and Australia Day was just about cooked. Nirvana had left love bites on the virgin city, and the gang wandered home in a daze. Tora had generously prepared a simple meal for everybody. He wanted to re-strike his return, and gather the pack over a feast that would offer a window of understanding to the cost of his absence.

The table was laden with more food than any of them had seen in weeks. Oli, Racer and Skinny huddled at one end where the roast chicken lay, like a golden sacrifice to the surfers. Jay was sitting too close to Ash, and Tora placed himself opposite her.

Ash had been reduced to a shell that day, despite the beguiling oceanic reprise that, in the end, cost her dearly. Tora observed her in every detail, as her eyes stayed magnetised to the cluttered tabletop. His attention felt like warm sunlight, and Ash was not well versed in how to shield herself from the comfort it gave her. She knew all too well that any display of pleasure would be a fatal blow to Jay's equilibrium.

It was a relief that, by this stage, Skinny and Oli were eating the chicken like pigs, forcing Ash to watch the spectacle while trying to suppress her nervous laughter. She quickly reined herself in, and again sat meekly, trying to shrink under the table. Looking for the next distraction, Ash took a sip of beer from her chipped blue mug.

Tora watched her mouth draw in the amber. His heart raced as she spilled a little. She involuntarily licked the escaped beer from her bottom lip, catching the rest on her chin with her slender, unloved hand.

'Where do you live Ash?' Tora tried to sound detached as Ash licked her lips once more.

'Well... I live here now,' Ash was unsure of the right answer, given the stiff greeting she had witnessed outside earlier and looked to Jay for guidance.

'But I'm from the Southern Highlands. I grew up there, and the Snowy Mountains. I just arrived on the coast a few months ago.'

'And how's that going?' Tora, perturbed as his fears of Ash's entrenchment were confirmed.

'I—' Ash tried to speak but Jay cut her off.

'She loves it. We haven't really gotten out there yet. Just the beach and—' in turn, Tora cuts Jay off in quiet defence of Ash.

'You surf?'

'No... not yet. I mostly watch Jay surf when I'm down the beach... he's so good.'

'Uh huh,' Tora grunted under his breath and finished his beer with one gulp.

'I'm good on a skateboard though. I used to compete before...'

Ash drifted away from her sentence and Jay, stunned at this new information that Ash was a professional skateboarder, left him annoyed. Oli started giggling, lighting up the table with his beaming smile, elated, and leaving no room for tension.

While Jay was looking to his comrades, Tora made contact with Ash. All at once, he remembered Ash from the magazine cover. *It was her.* She looked broken, but he was sure it was her. She had helplessly wandered into La Quinta, bewitched by Jay. Tora was struck. Ash forcibly shifted from his trance and kept her eyes down as she stared again, at her chipped blue mug.

'I've got a Powell Peralta,' Tora almost stammered. 'If you wanna use it? Whenever you want,' he held his breath.

'Thanks man, but I don't think she's into it these days. She hasn't skated since she's been here,' Jay, back in the conversation, broke the spell.

Ash shrunk further into her restrained posture, trying to camouflage her sadness as she reflected on her lost skateboard, and the undeniable excitement Tora's look generated at her core, only to add to her confusion.

'How was Japan?' Jay forced the subject to change.

'Great,' Tora was bored with this.

'Tora is a hyperbaric welder,' Jay continued.

'Umm, that's underwater welding right? My Dad told me about it when I was a kid. He was designing a bridge and trying to explain everything to me technically... so sweet, now that I think about it,' Ash wandered backwards in time, and lower into her seat.

'Not anymore. I bet you're missing the mountains,' Tora was right there with her, unconsciously lowering to her level.

Ash bowed her head in response, with a smile of assent. Tora cleared his throat and abruptly stood to leave the table with his finished plate.

'We'll clear this later,' he announced, as if dismissing the boys from the dining room. He disappeared into the flame orange kitchen.

Ash, Jay and the three boys sat poolside under the moonlight. Oli was curled asleep on a deck chair like a puppy.

'Looks like it's time to get ripped. Who's up for it?' Jay said in a low voice as he lit up a joint he had been working on for the past several minutes.

'Fuck yeah. Sweet,' Racer was in.

'Yep. Bring it on,' Skinny was in.

Oli semiconsciously raised a hand. He was in too.

'That's a trifecta!' Jay laughed. 'Let's go do this on the lounge. These chairs suck.'

All the guys traipsed inside, even Oli managed to get up off the old deck chair to go in. He'd always follow a joint, like a carrot on a stick.

Much to her relief, Ash was left alone by the pool. Just her and the yawning moon. The night was still and humid. It was filled with the scent of the frangipani tree by the pool. Ever since Ash had arrived in Spring, it had groaned with flowers that would spin themselves like island dancers onto the surface of the water—at the slightest hint of a breeze. Ash lifted her sundress and slowly stepped into the dark leafy water.

Tora watched Ash from the door while keeping check on the boys getting stoned in the lounge room. He wasn't sure what to do next, but he did know there would be close to zero chance of getting Ash alone, as long as Jay was around. Tora stepped outside and close to the edge of the pool. He watched Ash float on a faded Pool Pony as she dipped her face into the water, holding her breath as long as she could. She seemed to be content just drifting, oblivious to Tora watching her, entranced by her graceful form.

Tora decided to take a chance. He dropped into the pool without a ripple, immersing himself completely. For what seemed like forever to Ash, he remained submerged. Tora surfaced close to her as she bobbed on her once jolly inflatable pony, faded and pink. He looked up to the sky, avoiding immediate eye contact with her. He wanted his presence to feel unobtrusive and whisper quiet. He wanted her to feel safe, which he knew was a stretch in this house.

'How many full moons have you been here, Ash?' his voice lightly travelled the surface of the water that separated them.

'Three,' Ash looked up to the moon as well.

'Don't you miss home?'

'Yes... no... I don't know... I can't find it.'

'And where's your pink hair?'

'How do you know?' Ash changed her tone, and her eyes darkened. 'That girl is gone.'

Tora was too close to her now, and he recognised her. The long day had over delivered to all Ash's senses, insecurities and desires. With one definite stroke of her tired arms, she paddled backwards, distancing them.

Before Tora could say anything, Ash glanced away to see Jay watching them. She slid off the Pool Pony and swam to the edge, and Jay disappeared back into the house. Ash walked back inside, dripping wet, without turning back.

Tora glided his hand along the surface of the water, tracking the rippled moonlight and then he sank.

Ash passed the stoned boys on the couch unnoticed, and went upstairs to grab a fresh change of clothes and a towel. She looked forward to a hot shower, which seemed the only thing that might wash the long day away. On her return downstairs she stopped on the top step. Her heart pounded when she heard Tora's raised voice, and then Jay's retaliation. She descended a few more steps to see exactly what was going on. Through the balustrade, Ash watched as Tora, soaked, and Jay, baked, stood toe to toe in confrontation, like warriors measuring their opponent before combat.

'Hey man, that's not what this is!' Jay yelled defiantly.

'It's exactly like before. What do you think's gonna happen next Jay? Tell me.'

'She's big enough to deal with whatever shit goes down,' Jay was being pushed into a familiar corner, he knew it. 'The door's open... she can do whatever,' he added.

'The door's open? Like the *other one*? And where is she? Huh?... We'll never know will we Jay?' Tora glowered.

'Stay away from Ash,' Jay dared to point a finger to Tora's chest.

Ash clenched her jaw as she bravely walked downstairs and through the middle of the room and the argument. The air was thick, and Jay didn't acknowledge Ash when she entered. She watched them listlessly for a long pause before finally speaking.

'I'm taking a shower,' she meekly announced to Jay before immediately turning and walking towards the bathroom.

'Hey baby, okay,' Jay's voice eventually followed her as she closed the bathroom door. She ran the water, as their yelling continued to penetrate the walls.

'You're unbelievable. Get out there and pick up the fucking glass before somebody gets hurt. I don't want the dog to walk on it. You should've done it hours ago!' Tora ordered.

'Yeah okay. Whatever. It's dark. Good idea. Fuckin' idiot. Fuck you Tora!' Jay yelled a moment before the front door slammed.

In the shower, Ash leant against the wall and found herself needing to cry. The day, the week, the month, the year, had taken its toll on her. All she wanted to do was disappear. Edie used to say '*Nothing would ever be thrown at you that you can't handle.*' Ash believed it religiously, until now.

Ash rested a razor blade in her hand and watched it collect beads of water. Her finger pressed on the edge of the blade and drew a drop of rosy red blood. The colour struck her as it contrasted her lily palm, and she waited until all the blood washed away. Ash knew she couldn't do it. She knew she didn't want to hurt herself, she wasn't ready to die. She put the blade on the shower shelf and took off her bikini. She concentrated on changing her thoughts by tipping her head back and closing her eyes, letting the water roll bead by bead down the length of her warming body.

Without permission, she was already thinking of him. She was finally able to put a face to the name, and that handsome dark figure she had been wondering about since she first set foot in La Quinta. It felt awkward and wrong, but Ash had justified that it was alright to follow her impulses since the only privacy she had left was in her imagination, and Jay couldn't take that from her. She felt like she had known Tora as long as she had known Jay. They all spoke of him often, and it sounded like he had given each of them a solid foundation to work from when they were most in need, especially Jay.

Ash felt goosebumps rise across her breasts as the water suddenly cooled. She kept her eyes closed and let her imagination wander for a stolen moment. She wondered what it would be like to paddle in the golden surf with Tora. *Probably really amazing,* she interrupted herself. They'd drop from their surfboards into the aquamarine and he would joyfully embrace her. Everything would slow down as they kissed, then Ash would playfully swim away, looking up to see the underside of their two surfboards drifting side by side in the deep. The refracting sun would touch their skin in warm wings of light.

Ash was jolted to reality with an abrupt knock on the bathroom door. She ignored it, until she heard Tora's loud whisper.

'Ash, let me in. Quick,' Tora pleaded apologetically. 'I'm sorry. I need a chance to talk to you... alone.'
'No. Are you kidding?'

A brisk bang! and the bathroom door opened and just as quickly, it closed again. Tora had boldly pushed the door open and entered Ash's steamy sanctuary. Ash couldn't believe his audacity, her mouth open with surprise, she instinctively tried to cover herself, even though she was behind the opaque shower door.

He sat on the edge of the tub, beside the shower.

'You don't belong here,' he started. 'Jay's done this before and it's never gonna stop.'

Ash was bemused as he settled into his monologue, 'But maybe he just needs more. More love,' she said with softness.

'I've been trying for a long time Ash, he's never going to give you all of him. He's broken,' Tora stalled. 'He lost her... his first love,' and continued after a long echoed pause, 'In the surf. A year ago. They went at night, they'd been drinking. He came home alone. Nobody will ever know what really happened out there. She's gone. Nebraska's dead.'

Ash's heart sank into the grim reality of what Tora was carefully explaining.

'You gotta go, soon. It would be wrong for me to let this slide. Jay has a history. I'll pave the way, make you some room. You gotta free yourself Ash. Go home,' he stood and moved back to the door. 'Please,' he added.

Tora left the bathroom with a quiet click. Ash paused with a guttural 'Oh God' before turning off the faucet. She stepped out of the shower and tightly wrapped herself in a towel. When Ash opened the bathroom door, she was taken aback to see Jay standing at the threshold waiting for her like a snarling hungry dog.

'We're outta here in a few days,' he growled. 'For good. Make sure you're ready.'

Ash, red eyed and exhausted by the episodic day, nodded to him in acceptance. She courageously pushed past Jay and he grabbed her. She defiantly pulled away from him and walked up the hallway to their bedroom. She'd pay for that.

CHAPTER TWELVE

Good Times Bad Times

At sixty-one, James Knight was a weary looking man. He wore his hair long and wiry, like frayed steel wool. It stiffly landed just past his shoulders in a trio of rusted colours. James imagined his long wild hair made him appear more attuned to his youthful lust for life. *Oh, if only they knew, these young foals, what a wild one I was. I could ride all night. All night long,* he would recite to himself as he walked, limping slightly, through the throngs of stripped bare women on the boardwalk. But James had lost the battle with gravity and struggled to accept it each time he caught his reflection, always surprised that he did not look as young as he felt.

A man of small stature, James now stood as tall as his spine would allow, extending his bare chest as he faced his empty bed in the decrepit, sparse room that was lit by one omnipresent bulb. A purple glow pulsed from the neon sign outside the Palm Beach Lodge like a butchers light. The noisy hum of intermittent traffic just below the window weighed on the mood, and James deeply inhaled the fumed air. He strolled to the old free standing oak wardrobe and pulled the doors wide open, releasing the stench of moth-balls an overzealous land-lord had planted. James had made his selection earlier in the afternoon, and now it was time to get ready for his night of nights.

He carefully laid out a suit of deep purple on the crooked mustard bedspread and smoothed it over, stroking it like a magical Persian cat. The fabric looked like real velvet and had an aura all of its own. It was his only suit, and fortunately, it was also James' lucky suit. He added a matching shirt to his outfit that was the colour of pink fairy floss. He stood back to admire the grand ensemble before him, as he had time and time before.

James paused and endured a few guttural coughs before he buttoned his shirt, tied back his hair and checked his crooked eggshell smile in the book-sized mirror on the wall. It was routine for James to sing to himself as he prepared to go out, occasionally bopping his head and mumbling the words of some of the greatest rock songs, he thought, were ever made.

'da da dah da loving you baby...' he sang with the tempo of a lullaby in his husky voice.

Now all set to hit the streets, James killed the light, coughed once or twice, and reached for his dice keyring. He quietly hoped that when he returned he would be a changed man, that tonight would be the night.

Someone his boy could be proud of. Jay had been a tough kid to please since James got out a few years back.

The real reason Jay harboured issues with his Father was plain to see. Jay's Mother passed away from a heroin overdose when he was four. Jay stayed by his dead Mother's side for three days before wandering out onto the front yard, to the neighbours horror. Nobody was there for Nora in the end, only baby Jay. Nora was all but a child herself when Jay was born. At only sixteen and a runaway, she drifted into the wrong man's arms and then quietly passed away. It didn't help that James was convicted of robbery when Jay was just a powder blue bundle. They sent James off to Long Bay for thirteen years. Maybe he could have saved Nora, but 'A man's gotta eat,' James would always say.

Down at the Golden Nugget Bar, James felt like a king. He'd been a VIP member for six months, ever since he had a flurry of small wins. James had a certain way about him, the way he moved. He had a strut, and walked to a beat nobody else could hear, but he also had a limp. The combination made him appear frail somehow, but in his mind, he was fierce. Walking along an aisle of poker machines chanting and beckoning, James was strutting and singing as his eyes darted from one poker machine to the next.

'Who's going to be the lucky lady tonight?' James murmured.

A younger couple passed by and the man awkwardly

bumped into James. He immediately turned to apologize. James paused and then turned with a deliberate smile, showing all those eggshell teeth and started singing again, only louder, before he pushed the man as hard as he could. James continued on his way. Nobody was going to ruin his night.

James was half sitting on a barstool at a poker machine, fully engaged in his gambling which was only interrupted by painful coughing. People were all around. Men had smartly combed their hair and added belts to their knee-length, tailored shorts, and the ladies were excited to be out in their fruity summer frocks and bouncy fresh perms. James looked from another time and place with his purple lounge suit. As he fed tokens into the machine, he continued singing that *Kiss* song he'd been playing is his head all day. '...and tonight,' he crooned.

He paused to get another handful from his plastic cup and fed a token into the Game King. He continued singing. Of course, without warning, all bells and whistles were set off and raised the roof! All the lights flashed like sirens in Hell's Kitchen, James had finally won the Golden Nugget Jackpot! *Forty grand.*

'I knew you'd put out for me baby!' James cheered before he excitedly kissed the poker machine.

Moreen Barber, a rotund drinks waitress who had worked at the Golden Nugget Bar since James moved to the Gold Coast, was passing by during the excitement. James looked at her in disbelief to share his incredible moment.

'Forty thousand dollars! Mr.Knight, After all these years... congratulations,' she cheerfully gushed.

'Thanks, darling. C'mon, give the winner a kiss,' he said hurriedly, lapping up the excitement.

James embraced Moreen, who was a few inches taller than him, and more abundant in every way. He kissed her, grabbing her around the waist, as much as he could manage, until she started to squeal with delight.

'Mr.Knight!'

'Ha!ha! My lady. It's time to celebrate. Shall we? Will you be my lady tonight?'

'Oooh. Yes!'

James started to slow dance in a dome of rainbow light as a small crowd formed around him on the psychedelic carpet. He felt special, like a Messiah. He did enjoy an audience.

The Surfers Paradise coastline stretched thinly under the skin coloured sky. Lights softly glowed in the distance, hovering within the dark band of concrete blocks. James' weathered face, framed with his now greasy hair, rested meditatively as he reflected on the cool sand. He'd seen a thing or two in his time. He slowly ate a soft-serve cone. His tongue curled the icecream like an animal being fed through the narrow bars of a zoo enclosure, grappling for more. James thought it was delightful that he could even get icecream by the sea at six in the morning. Damn, he loved this place. He was still wearing his lounge suit, which he would typically find upsetting. Sand was so hard to get out of velvet, he found. James was thinking all of this while gazing intently towards the waves as they lapped sleepily. In front of him, he had neatly laid out a handkerchief which cushioned several wads of cash on the sand, and seductively beside it, Moreen's discarded waitress uniform.

In the distance, the object of his desire, was swimming. Moreen's shrill as she submerged into the blue struck James out of his trance. She was in her under wear, feeling sexy and alive. More alive than she could ever recall. Her enormous white briefs and matching sensible bra, mixed with the excitable froth of the sea, as she launched her body, made for quite a sight.

When James was finally able to peel his eyes away from Moreen's transparent underwear, he looked at the pile of cash before him and thought he should be serious this time, not blow it. Set a good example for Jay by turning over a new leaf. *Maybe even settle down with her. She seemed like a high quality lady. Maybe she could bake for me. Maybe she doesn't snore and could keep me company night after night... a man's gotta eat.* James thought as Moreen breached.

CHAPTER THIRTEEN

Breaking The Girl

Floating in the sunlight that peeked through the curtains, were iridescent dust particles, one more lovely than the next. It was in these moments Ash now found wonder. She sat on the bed in her underwear, sucking hungrily on a ripe orange quarter with a pen in her hand, as she scanned the room for evidence of magic. The shadows shape-shifted like x-rays on the yellow wallpaper, as the palm tree outlines and reflections of the swimming pool water below, danced in splashes, gilt by the light. Glimpses of golden sunshine beckoned and were broken by Jay's hunched frame on the roof. Ash spontaneously wrote as she drifted to Tora with her black pen poised.

'I now live in a beautiful dark secret.
I have never felt so alive, and so filled with emptiness.
Loving you was never a choice. You're trapped in my veins.
When will our day come?'

Jay sat on the roof edge, smoking. Arms length from him, the *Other One* sat, mirroring Jay's position, with her legs dangling. She was still naked, and her hair fell low, brushing the blistering tin as she swayed. Ash felt a rush of jealousy flush her cheeks. *How did she get up on the roof, our roof? Naked? And nobody mentions a thing about it? Why does she call herself the Other One? The Other what?* Ash had no answers to give herself for now. All she knew was her and Jay were out of La Quinta in less than a week, and Tora was home, throwing her into a spin... and now this, out on the roof. This girl. This strange, strange girl.

Jay's heart-shaped mouth compressed as he dragged on his joint, slowly drawing back and then exhaling a palm tree of smoke, feeling the sun on his tired face. The *Other One* turned to look at Jay once more and pushed her thick mane behind her pallid seashell ear. She glanced back towards the house, with her cellophane green eyes crackling, catching Ash's stare, unflinchingly.

'I've tried to talk to you a thousand different ways,' The *Other One* began in a melted tone. 'Your voice is my home. It brings my smile, even if you are the reason it's gone,' she chanted. '*Your beauty penetrates my skin like heat.* You said that to me once,' her poetics fell on deaf ears and she bowed her head sorrowfully.

Jay stood and stretched his arms to their full athletic extension, holding his position with closed fists for a moment, before he realigned and looked out to the horizon. He closed his eyes and listened to the sea.

'Don't you love me, Jay? You said you would love me forever. You said *Nebraska, Nebraska, Nina! I wish I could live inside you, or keep you in my pocket.* Don't you remember?' she too, stood up and stilled her body like a divine marble statue. Only her hair gave way to the breeze that was collecting the afternoon.

There she was, like a diety, immortal, Nebraska Parkes, a high priestess, The *Other One*—next to Jay on that hot tin roof. Jay oblivious to the presence of his one great love, turned away and flicked the remainder of his joint into the looming palm grove.

Nebraska, devastated by her predicament, took one step forward, then another, dropping off the rooftop in silent protest, and out of Ash's sight.

'No!' Ash caught herself shouting in reflex.
'No what!? Will, you shut up Ash. Never any peace,' Jay snapped at volume.

The window next to the bed was open wide, and Jay climbed back into his cave. He stood over Ash on the bed and stared at her without emotion. Ash tried to hide her anxiety and gave a meek smile as she slid her notebook beneath her.

'Why are you so pale? Are ya sick?' Jay asked coldly, his eyes almost aqua in the light.
'I'm fine,' Ash assured him.
'Where were ya before, when I was with Racer in the shaping bay?' he flatly asked.
'Here.'

'I know you were here. Where in the house? While I was downstairs?' he pressed.

'I took a shower,' Ash whispered.

'And where else? Don't you lie to me, you stupid bitch,' he murmured without blinking.

Jay's fury quickly escalated, and he dropped to his knees, straddling Ash. He watched her for a moment as she looked back to him, trying to imagine why he couldn't see Nebraska, nor sense her... or maybe he could sense her subconsciously, and that's why he was so angry all the time. Ash was not about the solve the mystery.

Jay gripped his hands around Ash's throat, and pinned her to the bed, just enough to scare her and let her fight for air a moment. Ash felt her throat close for the first time in her life and was gasping with futility. She overthrew her instincts, she knew better than to fight back. *So it's true. He loved Nebraska so much he couldn't stand her being alive. He had to possess her so wholly and absolutely, that death was the only place for her safekeeping. Was this how the mind of a killer worked?* Ash let her thoughts smash through her mind as she took what might have been her last moments. At least she would be with Edie now, and she had just seen a ghost. Ash hoped she would have ethereal beauty like Nebraska in the afterlife... she drifted.

'No more of him. Understand? No more!'
He menaced, in a low growl, to her breathless face as he shook Ash's weakened body further into the bed.

Ash closed her eyes, she was ready to go. There was a peaceful smile resting on her face, and Jay realised he had gone too far. He released his hold on her throat. In silence and without the usual dramatic performance, he left the room, leaving his girl in shock.

The room felt still. She was still alive. The kitten was still sleeping in the corner on a pile of magazines, and the magpies were still chortling. Ash had a second chance. She shot to her feet scared and enraged, and without hesitation, briskly started to pack her cotton bag before hiding it under the bed. She was ready to go.

Ash heard Jay pacing back up the hall towards her. She leapt back onto the bed and found her composure, she was used to it by now. Ash realised she was in a compromised position, but wanted out. She decided to continue complying with Jay while she worked towards her own freedom. She was vulnerable still, with no money at all and under complete control for twenty-four hours a day. For now, grave danger was her lot, but her eyes were wide open to his manipulation.

'I'm sorry baby. I'm so sorry. Hold me? I'm so tired. I love you. Can you forgive me, baby?' Jay begged with his softest voice. He gently put his hands on hers, and drew her in and kissed her as soft as a dusted marshmallow. 'All the guys are downstairs. Tora rented a video. *Point Break* or somethin'. The movie's gonna start in a minute. Let's go down'n watch it, spend some time together. You can rest.'

Ash nodded blankly and followed him lethargically as he lead her by the hand.

Johnny Utah and Bodhi were about to smash into Anthony Kiedis and friends at the beach shower. Oli was full of fight sounds and Jay laughed so hard—he grabbed Racer's shoulder and told him to watch. Tora was half asleep, and Skinny crunched feverishly on salt and vinegar chips. The fight reminded Oli to pass on an essential message to Jay.

'Oh, Johnny's lookin' for ya.'
'That prick can wait, ay? He dropped in on me yesterday, I should'a smashed him. I fuckin' hate the guy,' Jay cursed.

Right on cue, an invasive chime blared through the room. The doorbell rang. *The doorbell... Who knew they had a doorbell,* Ash marvelled.

'Who is it?' Tora grumbled.
'Fuk Yu.' The outside voice called.

Tora smiled. The stoned triplets giggled in unison like animated hamsters that had just fallen off their wheel in a huddle.

'Better get your fifty bucks,' Skinny muttered to Jay.
'Fuck you!' Jay called as he reached for the remote control and stopped the film in frustration.

The front door opened. Johnny had shown up to pay the boys a visit. He let himself in and stood in front of the television. He looked at Jay, arms crossed, he rocked back on his heels with a hard tilt. His black wrap-around sunglasses and cleft chin gave him a menacing ambience.

'That's Detective Fuk Yu to you, you prick,' he said as he looked over to the smashed window that was sealed with plastic sheeting and gaffer tape.

Johnny moved from the television and walked past the couch, clipping Jay on the back of the head before sitting down hard and too close next to him. Johnny was intimidating to all the guys and remained unchallenged. He gestured his hand in front of Jay to pay up the money owed. Ash shuffled over and then finally stood up, looking for any reason to leave the cramped couch. Exactly as Johnny had intended.

'Babe, I'll go and... make a coffee,' she stumbled with her excuse.

'Yeah, whatever. I don't want one, so whatever,' Jay quipped.

As Ash left the room, Tora threw a look to Johnny who responded with a subtle nod. Johnny was going to hold the space for now. It was his pleasure and duty to keep Jay occupied so Tora could talk to Ash.

Ash mindlessly stared at the steam rising from the kettle, daydreaming of the outside world, one without Jay. She placed a hand on her tender throat to soothe herself and was reminded of the lucky Japanese looking coin she had discovered in the sea.

'Ash?' Tora startled her, and she turned to face him automatically. She watched his eyes, and then his mouth. 'Hey. Hi. I like your necklace. Is that fifty yen?' he had never had so much trouble to say the most simple things. 'Can you meet me tonight? By the pool? At nine? I'll be there. I'll wait. Jay won't be around, don't worry about that. I'll make sure he's distracted.'

Ash paused and took a moment to process his questions, there seemed so many. She wasn't fully paying attention either, so she made him wait, painfully so, while considering what to answer. It was an eternity for Tora. She delivered a slight curve in her smile, and tilted her head before shyly looking down to her bare feet. That's the only answer he needed. His heart was doing flips. *She was magic, like nothing else in the world.* Tora returned to *Point Break* with a persistent grin. He felt like doing a high kick, like Bodhi, but instead resumed his nap on the couch in the interest of passing time, as the afternoon inched closer to evening.

The film was over. Ash and Jay sat out on the roof in the tropical canopy of the back yard. The sunset had delivered mosquitos and Ash was being eaten alive. As Jay spoke, she scratched her skin to the point of drawing blood. She wished he would notice her sometimes, in the right way.

'Dad called. He won again at the pokies. Forty grand. He'll probably lose it all by next week. That's what usually happens.'
'That's a lot of money, *wow*.'

'He's givin me 'is car... I haven't seen 'im for ages.'

'That's so cool.'

'We're gonna pick it up later from his place.'

'Tonight? Oh baby, how about we go tomorrow morning? I'm so tired.'

'Nah. We're goin at eight. End'a story.'

Ash rested her mouth on her stinging knee. She bit down to distract herself from her burning skin.

CHAPTER FOURTEEN

Diamonds & Pearls

The weather had turned with the night. The sea rumbled and cast its spray like a spell across the wide Palm Beach street. Ash was sure to hold the handrail as she tracked Jay high up the damp staircase that creaked in the wind. They arrived at the top level of the sea bitten structure that leaned into the coast like a broken umbrella. When Jay knocked on the icecream coloured door, Ash stood well back. She waited behind him with apprehension, happily insignificant. A squall lifted the mouldy vintage awning to its extremes, and with that, Moreen Barber glamorously opened the door with a forced hand. Her head tipped back as she raised her gracious smile to the gale. Her frock danced around her bloated pink toes.

Moreen had struck gold. She was adorned with faux gem earrings that dangled like complicated parachutes, and a matching choker necklace that gripped her throat in anguish. Her fingers, each like a champagne flute, were sparking with lavish princess cut Alaska diamonds.

She wore an orotund evening gown that begrudgingly dragged on the ground behind her like a mistreated animal. Her perfume preceded her high voice as notes burst from those usually pursed apricot lips. She looked Jay up and down with hungry eyes.

'Hi. Umm,' Jay was lost.

'James! Where are yah, honey? He's here!' she screeched like a banshee. 'Come in Jay-Jay,' she suddenly adjusted her range and spoke with a coy undertone. '... and your friend.'

Ash and Jay crossed the threshold, escaping the temper of the weather, they stepped into the solemn flat. Inside was like a bare cupboard, humid and sleepy-eyed. The unit looked as if nobody lived there. The forties kitchen was quaint, even though it had a few broken panels that made the apartment look as though it had missing teeth. A pulsing glow crept in from the neon outside and consumed the bare floors in a wash of violet—just how James liked it.

James entered the kitchen grinning and barefoot. He carried himself proudly with a slight limp. His energy was sapped, and his blinking eyes pushed away folds of creased skin, crisped in the sun for perhaps sixty summers or more. His chest wheezed under his wife-beater. A deep cough stopped him at the threshold of the bedroom, and he clutched the doorframe as the wind whipped the rooftop. He refocussed before he spoke.

'Hello, I'm James. And who might this be?' he formally extended his hand with the slightest bow. He was charmed.

'Hi. I'm Ash. Nice to meet you.'

'Enchanté,' he smiled, just with the left of his mouth, showing his gap toothed charisma in just one breath. 'Ash? Can I call you Ashley? It's one of my favorite names.' He coughed and coughed.

'Yeah, sure.'

'Hello son—' his eyes not leaving Ash's form.

'Hi,' Jay impatiently greeted his Father.

James moved in much closer to Ash. She was noticeably taller than him, and she felt self-conscious as he peered at her windswept hair. Ash blushed as James reached out with two crooked fingers and collected a strand that kissed her shoulder.

'You're hair is so golden,' he hummed.

'Uhhh. Thanks. It gets a lot of sun,' Ash cheerfully replied to ease the tension vibrating from Jay.

'I bet it smells like coconut,' James continued, and gently let go of Ash's hair.

'Dad... don't do this,' Jay sighed, working hard to control his volcano.

'What? I like to say what I think. It's not a crime... Is it darlin'?' his eyes fixed on Jay's girl.

'Nope,' she said brightly, in a tone that would never appease the room.

Moreen had seen enough. She waddled to her man and wrapped a tall arm around his slight shoulders.

She hung off him like a cheap fur until James stepped forward to escape her grip. He buried a hand into his tattered trouser pocket and produced a car key with a dice keyring then held it dangling in the air like a carrot.

'Honey, Jamie baby, hold me... I...' Moreen drifted into a purr.

James, trying to ignore his girl, pushed her away, but she was stubborn like that and he felt like he was moving a fridge. In futility, James half heartedly put an arm around her constricted waist.

'Relax woman! I'm right here,' he quipped. 'I'm happy you got lucky... With your winnings, that is.'

James was now putting his attention to Jay as he motioned the keyring towards his son. Moreen, now hanging off him like a drunken sloth sighed with boredom.

'Jay-Jay, This is your big start son, don't blow it... go get a job. Build a life with your girl. The car is a real beauty. The ladies love it,' he winked.
'Wow... I'm sure I will,' Jay was trying not to sound underwhelmed by his Father's advice. 'It's getting late. We haven't eaten yet—'
'I'm ok if you want to stay awhile,' Ash unskilfully interrupted.

Jay glared at Ash, and she shrank her posture, realising her error.

'Yeah! C'mon, stay. Moreen will cook us a helluva pie. She makes pies.'

'No, no, we gotta go,' Jay was firm,

'It's been good to see you son. Maybe you can stop by again soon? Now you've got a car.'

'Yeah, alright. Bye, James,' he agreed, to keep civility.

Jay stuffed the keys into his jeans pocket and descended the stairs, fighting the dark howling wind, with Ash in tow.

'Well that was fun, couple of freaks,' Jay was drained.

'He's family.'

'Well, I didn't get to choose... I don't have a family.'

The couple arrived at a row of narrow garages. Number three was open, and Jay approached, brimming with caution and doubt. The tail of the car protruded just shy of the garage boundary, giving away its colossal scale. It fit in the garage like a bright basketball shoe, in a too-small box.

'And now I've got a purple car, for fuck's sake! Look at it!' Jay almost screamed.

Jay and Ash approached the car and tentatively climbed in, like astronauts unsure of their fate. The muggy atmosphere had bonded with every surface as a misty layer, leaving imprints with every touch. The car interior was nothing of the usual sort and had a homemade centre console, poorly crafted out of wooden wall panelling and finished with a box cutter, leaving sharp, ragged edges.

When Jay turned the ignition by a click, the dashboard didn't respond, and in his natural reaction to most of life's imperfections, he punched it.

'Well, maybe it runs really well,' Ash scraped for words.

The purple car begrudgingly started and the exhaust coughed into the blustering night. Jay fumbled to find his way with the unreasonably delicate gear shift. Clouded with anger, he clumsily reversed the car onto the street, slamming the tortured curb with the underbelly of his new ride. The engine was overwhelmingly loud. Jay turned on the radio to discover its silence and was by now, fuming.

'And who needs fucking music!? Hey? Answer me!'

Tapping the steering wheel hard, he started muttering under his breath and throwing glances at Ash. Then louder and louder, he recited a Henry Rollins song. As the new car hurtled up the beachside highway, Ash watched him, pretending to be interested, to avoid a fight. She looked at the clock. Nine, forty-four. She imagined Tora lying by the pool looking up at the clouded moon, waiting for her. Ash tipped her head back in disappointment and glanced to the side mirror only to see police lights flashing.

Jay also saw police lights hovering in the rearview mirror. Punching the dashboard again, in protest, he started turning the wheel to pull over.

'Now what? What the... fuck! C'mon! There's nowhere here to pull over.'

Jay didn't want any trouble from the cops. Not tonight. He pulled over at the nearest point on the median strip, which unfortunately grew into a steep slope of concrete. The purple car advanced along the median strip and came to a halt, tipping sideways in a ridiculous manner.

The car rested on the steep footing, and all was still. Jay killed the engine. Cars zoomed by, tooting and honking as the officer's boots approached Jay's window. When Jay saw the policeman's feet he wound down the window forcibly. The officer crouched down and bent his neck sideways to see into the tilted car window. Jay, red eyed and clenching his jaw with rage, was face to face with the law.

'Drivers license?'

Jay stiffened his body like a board and dug into his back pocket. He pulled out his license, and handed it upwards through the window.

'Mr. Knight.'
'Yes.'
'A fine spot you have there on Monaco Street canal.'
'It's alright.'
'Aren't you a slippery fellow? This purple beauty has almost two thousand dollars worth of traffic violations pinned to her.'

'Fuck!' he struck her dashboard again, sealing his bruise.

'You took a real gamble driving this car out tonight. Looking for trouble no doubt. Get out of the car Mr Knight.'

Jay undid his seatbelt and tried to open the door, but it hit the sloped pavement and could not open. Jay slammed the car ceiling with an urgent growl, like a trapped animal.

The officer stepped back, amused. Jay climbed out through the window and tumbled onto the street over-dramatising the situation, like he was four.

Eventually, the purple car was towed away. Eleven o'clock. Ash followed Jay as he stormed back to Monaco Street. The wind died down and midnight welcomed them home.

❧

Ash lay awake in bed with Jay in her arms as he slept heavily on her chest. She looked out at the night sky with sonder.

A warm melodic voice curled under the bedroom door. Music had begun to play softly. It drifted from Tora's room to Ash's cut open heart. *Pearl Jam. Oceans.* Ash started to weep. She knew the words, all of them. She knew what they meant, and the intention of every breath in-between every word. Tora could not have called out louder words of longing on this night and played the song for her twice. Ash closed her eyes and fell asleep under a sheet of salted tears.

Jay woke first and tenderly watched Ash sleep for a moment. He knew he could never make her happy. *Girls like her were always difficult.* He wished he didn't love her so much. Reminding himself of this set him off centre. He felt disturbed and got out of bed roughly, no longer wanting to be close to her. He opened the wardrobe to tend to his crop. His *garden*, as he preferred to call it.

'Your Ramones tee is still downstairs. I'll go get it,' Ash was suddenly awake and spoke into the pillow.
'Why do you fuck'n forget everything? Make me a coffee,' he couldn't help it.

The demonic cupid wants a coffee, Ash bitterly mouthed as she resisted to rise. Ash climbed out of bed with the weight of the world and sleepily left the bedroom dressed in just her underwear and a tee shirt.

Stumbling into the kitchen, she could see only one thing—Tora's shirtless form, as he washed dishes in the hot morning light. His muscular back was covered with a Japanese tattoo. The tiger's red mouth snarled, which lit its fierce hazel eyes. It seemed ready to pounce amongst luxurious green bamboo and golden sun rays, that extended across his broad shoulders, with a front paw in a blue stream that curled around the small of his back in intricate shades.

She paused. She had no choice—it was hard to move away, not backwards or forwards, from the honesty of her feelings. The soap bubbles gently bounced around his arms like spherical rainbows filled with hope. Ash was stone, mesmerised, it seemed so long since she last saw something as beautiful. Tora threw a knife in the air and skilfully caught it, like an erotically charged circus act, it was all in slow motion. Longingly, she held the silent space before she announced her presence.

'Hi,' she mentioned, soft and light as a feather.

'Mornin'' without fully turning around to look at her.

'I'm going to make coffee, want one?' her voice cracked.

Tora shook his head and continued the dishes in silence. Ash started the kettle which was already full and leaned her back against the kitchen counter as she adjusted her bed hair, holding it up high and rearranging it. At that moment Tora turned to Ash, her beauty crushed his long rehearsed sentence to nothing, it dissipated into clouds. He was insignificant in her sublime radiance. He was evanescent.

'I waited,' he said, unable to look into the sunlight of her. Tora approached Ash, carefully, painfully without touching.

'Why do you stay?' he continued to whisper to her milky feet.

Ash openmouthed, and breathless, had nothing for Tora and her arms dropped to her side. Her fingers sought refuge in the fumbled hem of her inside-out tee shirt. She bowed her head with melancholy.

'I couldn't–' she stammered.

'ASH!' Jay's jolt from upstairs brutally sliced the exchange, bringing a dreaded silence.

Ash looked up to Tora, but he'd chosen to walk away. She turned to the coffee cup as the kettle sung its high pitch, which she let wail for the longest, loudest time. Her hands shaking, Ash carried the rippling drink back to the bedroom, slow as a funeral procession. There she remained for the day, while Jay went out searching for a new place to live. *Somewhere just for two.*

CHAPTER FIFTEEN

Blood Sugar Sex Magik

The bonfire raged. A yard of girls, with giggling silhou-ettes, encircled the dancing flames with hollow eyes. They closed in on the heady boys who clutched their beer with anticipation. It had been a while since there was a party at La Quinta. The pretty Monaco Street dollhouses closed their shutters and braced for a storm.

Johnny slouched next to Tora. He sank into his heat-flaked leather jacket as his long legs stretched forward from a too-small sun chair. All the others were barely dressed. Nebraska lay naked on the hammock, asleep in the frolicking shadows, and ignored by the party.

Ash and Jay gazed at the orange fire, shoulder to shoul-der, as it lit the pleasure seeker's faces like Halloween. Across the flames, Ash watched a young woman stare at Jay intently. She sat with her thick legs relaxed, in a mini skirt that stopped not too far below her waist. The voluptuous blonde girl noticed that Ash was all eyes.

She stood up, turned her back to the bonfire and bent over with a heavy lean of her hips, collecting a cider from the esky. Maddie hoped Jay was also watching since she was naked under that mini skirt. She knew he'd enjoy that.

Maddie stared back at Ash fireside, and twisted the top off her drink like the snap of a small bird's neck, before drawing it to her pouting lips. She circled the fire as Racer threw a dead tree onto the ravenous pyre, sending a flurry of sparks to the clouds. Maddie approached Jay with boldfaced lust, leaving Ash a phantom in her own story.

'I didn't know you'd be 'ere tonight,' Maddie smouldered as she closed in and put her hands on his tan-lined hips, drawing him in. Jay looked stunned by her brashness. 'Wanna go for a walk?' she said.

'No, who the fuck'r ya?' Jay slurred.

'C'mon Jay-Jay,' Maddie purred.

She reached to kiss him before Jay eased her away, trying to make light of the situation in front of Ash by rolling his eyes and laughing in a too- high pitch.

Tora watched from across the yard as deceit unfolded all around Ash. He knew Jay cheated on Ash with that girl—it's what he did. Ash now knew it too, and looked to Tora before backing away from the inferno, away from Jay.

Ash walked up the dizzying staircase and followed the aquamarine carpet to their bedroom. She collapsed in a heap on the dishevelled bed. Her melon pink dress smelled like charcoal and wanton desire. Ash hated parties. She breathed in the stillness of the room. Outside, voices and music escalated into a rumble, bouncing from the sleepy canal rooftops.

Jay's bedroom door closed behind Tora, clasping in the slow darkness. Ash sat up, wanting to conceal her wretched face, and covered her eyes with smokey fingers. Tora moved in carefully, gently holding her wrists, exposing her rawness. Ash followed his gesture, lifting from the bed in that dulled room, that cave, that cage.

The charged silence was held by Tora for as long as he could bear to look into her withering eyes, and soon enough, he extinguished her tears with his soft presence. His gentle breath warmed her blonde crown.

'I just need to clear my head—' she tried to speak, but her voice petered, then he held a finger to her lips.
'Follow me,' he hushed.

Tora took a step back with his eyes fixed to hers and then turned to open the bedroom door. They swiftly crossed the hall onto the deep pile carpet of his sanctuary, the master bedroom. Door locked.

In Tora's room, the streetlight outside washed against the large window and softly outlined their forms. It was quiet on this side of the house. The canal didn't echo every drunken holler, and the music was slow to eat into the air.

'I feel so hurt... so stupid, I just wish I had the sunshine part of him,' Ash continued.

'The sunshine? Ash, he's only got a small glimmer of sunshine and he's spent it pulling you in this deep.'

'That's all I wanted,' she sighed. 'And look at the mess I'm in. It's all my fault. I let this happen.'

'That what he's relying on Ash. He may love you, that would be easy to do, but he'll never be able to express it as a whole person. He's just broken, and now... well, look at you. What do' ya have left? You're magic. You are. I knew it the first time I saw you on Monday. It's only Thursday, and you've turned my world sideways... I can see you're getting wrung out, more and more,' he breathed out to finish. 'There's no time left.'

'I'm broke. I'm in danger if I stay, and I feel like it's even more dangerous to leave. If he finds me, which he eventually will, he'll kill me. I know it. He said if I leave him, he'll hurt my parents and their home and then me. I believe him.'

Tora looked to the ceiling in disbelief. Jay was a piece of work, that he knew, but now he could see the rawness of fear that was generated in Ash. It was devastating. Without processing the consequences, Tora was quick to speak.

'Tomorrow morning I'll take you home. I'll drive you there myself and we can talk all the way...

I'll even make a mix tape tonight for the trip,' he tried to lighten the weight of his invitation.

'It's a fourteen hour drive Tora. The Highlands are way past Sydney. I'm so far from home—and I don't even know if they ever want to see me again. There's a lot you don't know about me.'

'It doesn't matter,' he urged. 'Ash, look at me,' holding her tiny face in his hands. 'I can't bear to see you here, with him, I can't. It's time to go. A fresh start.'

Ash looked at him, so softly. She had never been held like that by a man before. It was deeply intimate and her shyness pulled her back a step.

'In the morning, meet me. In the kitchen. Six am. We'll be outta here in two minutes flat. He'll never know what happened. I'll handle things here when I get back,' Tora assured her.

'So, just like that... I'm gone? It's not that simple. It's a trap. It's all is a trap. It's like my very own Appointment in Samara.'

'What do you mean?'

'Nothing. Sorry. It's a story Edie told me just before she died... the inevitability of it all.'

'It's simple Ash. I want to take you home, and I will, no matter what. Straight to your door. You can lead the way and I'll make safe passage. No traps,' Tora promised.

'I don't need saving like this. I just need time, and I know I can sort things out here with Jay and calm him down, and help him, and then quietly walk away.'

'You know that's not true Ash. There's nothing to fix. This is it. You just said it a minute ago. He's a danger to you. As kind hearted and patient as you are, you won't be taming Jay… and besides, maybe I just want to take a long drive with you,' again, hoping he can squeeze her enough to agree.

Ash stood in Tora's sanctuary, everything was so still. She reflected.

'Who's going to water your bonsai when you're away?' Ash now playing his game.
'I was wondering how it survived so well.
I thought it was a miracle,' he took her hands. 'Maybe it was,' he drew her closer and she bowed her head. It was all too much, he kissed her forehead and released her.
'See you in the kitchen at six.'

Ash couldn't have loved Tora any more in that moment.

Her heart was aching to embrace him and fold herself into his waiting arms. And with that she silently left the room and returned to her opened cage across the hall.

The party was long over and Jay walked with Oli down Monaco Street under the low street lights, towards the egg-carton strip mall. By now it was two in the morning, with not a soul in sight. They walked past the bakery that had flamboyant birthday cakes proudly displayed in the window, like a sugar coated parade of hats on Race Day.

'I'm starvin'.'
'Shuddup man.'

Oli took a staggered leap, and slammed his shoulder into the bakery window, in a drunken attempt to smash through it.

'Oli! Fuckin' stop it,' Jay pleaded.

Oli punched the window in frustration and bent over laughing at the futility of his robbery attempt. Then, to add humour, he did it once more, and to his shock and then delight, the window shattered. It fell in large shards, like broken teeth in a cartoon, crashing to the chewing gummed pavement.

'Cakes! Oh man! In Dee Why we used to get cakes all the time!' Oli put his arm through the void and grabbed a small yellow cake decorated with marzipan bumblebees.

Jay looked up and down the vacant strip mall thoroughfare before climbing through the broken window. Catlike, with his invisible tail mischievously curling with anticipation of the kill, he pounced the cash register and skilfully prized it open—*two grand*. The purple car was saved.

∞

Jay crept through his bedroom window. Ash's form lay perfectly still, she appeared asleep until she slowly spoke into the darkness.

'Who was that girl?' she cut straight to it.

'What girl?'

'You know exactly. The girl that was all over you tonight. The one showing you her fat ass,' Ash sat up, making out Jay's frame in the night's glow.

'I dunno. She was super drunk, aye?'

'Well she seemed to know you.'

'Yeah, weird.'

'Were you with her?'

'No. I was with Oli in town.'

'I mean, anytime. Did you sleep with her?' Ash felt nauseous.

'Yeah. Yeah I did,' he exhaled. 'When you were being a total bitch.' He stepped onto the bed, closer to his girl, and pinned her down. His face close to hers with a diamond hard stare. 'So?'

Ash was speechless. His intensity suspended her racing mind.

'You're pathetic. Spineless. No point wasting time here with you... such a fuckin' waste of space.'

With a thorough push of her dark shoulders into the lumpy bed, he confirmed Ash's intention with bruises. He released her aggressively, wild with anger, and stormed out of the room. Ash counted... eight, nine, ten. The front door slammed. He was gone. So was she. He made it easy.

Five in the morning. Ash crouched beside the night before's fire pit as it smouldered with volcanic colours.

Like a dying dragon, tired sparks flinched as she drove a branch into its side, one last time. The yard of girls had abandoned, except for Nebraska. The night was endless for her, and in protest of her purgatory, she stood with her pearlescent feet on the wide bed of embers—a fire walker without ceremony.

'Today is the change.' She announced with breathy authority, perfumed with frankincense and myrrh.

Ash watched as the beautiful creature dissolved into the dawn like sugar in water. *I never want to be cremated, I want to sleep in the arms of an old tree, a warm limbed Mother, there until the end, like Edie.* Ash had thought of death often the past few days, as it presented itself again and again in fresh forms. And soon a new death, with just one hour to go, all of this would be over. Ash felt assured she'd fare better than Nebraska as she turned to leave the yard. She had surrendered her dissolved love for Jay to the fire—and the weeping grip of La Quinta. Ash climbed back to the rooftop, agile as a monkey, to gather her things and wait for six.

The bedroom looked more claustrophobic than before. The yellow wallpaper reminded her of an abandoned asylum, damp with despair. Her bag was packed small and waited under the bed. Ash sat in meditation, so nervous and ready, waiting for her ride home with Tora. She wondered if he really did make a mixtape. She imagined a golden breeze grazing the car as they'd hurtle through the open landscape, chasing the sun all the way home—the soundtrack, for sure, would be perfect.

Ash had a photo in her pocket, her hidden treasure. It had softened with white creases, like yesterday's newspaper. Slightly blurry, it framed Ash and Edie, as they held a birthday cake with burning candles, the twin's faces alight with smiles. Ash's pink hair bold and brilliant, cascaded to her waist, identical to Edie's, but hers as blue as the Pacific. The photo was inscribed with smudged biro on the back *'Edie & Ash, Feb, 1991. Happy Birthday girls - 20!'* It was impossible for Ash to not smile while giving the photo a little squeeze before sliding it back into her hip pocket.

The first crow cried in the day, without reply. Ash waited for the next sound, usually a Pied Currawong, proud and competitive. She would miss those birds. The house was silent, then the next sound came with a shrill.

'The pigs!' Oli yelped from downstairs.

A dog's bark came from outside, and the rumble of an urgent voice stopped time. Ash remained at the foot of the bed, under the window, frozen. There was a discreet knock on the bedroom door before it immediately opened. A policeman was at the threshold of Ash's open-doored cage.

'My name is Constable Ross. What's your name miss?'
'Ash.'
'Ashley?'
'Ashley Smith, sorry.'
'Miss Smith. Is this your room?' he calmly enquired.

'Yes. No, not really. Umm, yes. I sleep here.'

He started looking around the room and half heartedly opened stiff drawers brimming with boy's junk. Ash chewed the inside of her dry mouth and awkwardly picked up Ninja without knowing what else to do as the tiny room was being turned upside down by the young cop. She sat on the all-knowing bed, conscious of her vulnerability, and waited for the wardrobe door to be opened like a raised guillotine. That wardrobe full of drugs she had never touched, Jay's Garden of Eden would be her end.

The policeman put his hand on the reluctant wardrobe door to open it and was interrupted by a commotion downstairs. A dog was savagely barking and the rumbling voice continued. *Was that Moose?* Ash didn't think he had it in him. *Such a good dog.*

'Control your dog!' a distant call of urgency pounded from downstairs.

The officer briskly left the room to help his partner, deserting Jay's garden without a second thought.

Ash was shaking as she climbed out onto the roof. La Quinta grew silent once again, and not a soul stirred for the longest time. Ash perched on the edge and observed the rooftops of the dollhouses as they sighed with relief, now that order was restored.

'They're gone...Uhh... I'm sorry about before. I think about losing you, and I just can't stand it. I love you so much. Ya know?' Jay's voice crackled thinly and crawled down her back.

'I know you do,' Ash spoke with dullness.

The silent air was polluted with Ash's fresh resentment. The tainted morning held its breath as Ash's eyes darkened and sunk back into their hollows.

'Close one, hey?' Jay smiled.

Ash nodded with distress, eyes closed and hands shaking as she clutched her knees.

'Tora was less lucky. They busted him. They took him away. I guess they found his stash.'

'I didn't know he kept drugs here?' she broke her breath.

'Neither did he.'

Jay left Ash with those three words and climbed back inside her cage, beckoning her.

Ash stood at the edge of the roof and looked to the distant gravel below. She wondered if she should free fall, like Nebraska, but instead collapsed back on her haunches under the swaying palm throngs—losing her will, but not her balance.

CHAPTER SIXTEEN

Wish You Were Here

The view stretched from the whiteout wilderness of the western horizon, in the form of a sleeping woman, all the way to the east, reaching out to nowhere, depending which way Johnny turned his cheek. On this day, the mountainous woman drew the cusp of a storm tight to her pagan shoulder.

His bedroom could have been a cell except for the panoramic view. A hollow hearth, padded with a bare mattress positioned on the floor with plush symmetry, a tan cashmere blanket paired with an egg-white feather pillow, beaten into the shape of a fortune cookie. Sometimes a candle laced with spice, sometimes a six-string, or the bones of an orphan seashell. Next to the unplugged telephone, his Beogram 6000 sank into the deep pile, turning *Wish You Were Here* with tortuous clarity. The needle dragged through the song, leaving scratches on Johnny's thoughts.

Most mornings were the same now, and Johnny (Hansuke) Sato, thought of his isolation and the hatred he harboured. Hatred: A nurtured emotion mechanically entrusted from one son to the next, along the inured Sato line. *Thirty-three generations,* his Mother always reminded him. The song persisted solemnly, as Johnny lifted from his mattress to join the strange parade outside.

The penthouse was lit with crisp morning, and the sea breeze clipped the shutters with the scent of a mariner's catch. Distant gulls squabbled to an escalated pitch that hovered above the eaves, and the green sunlight broke as Johnny squinted into the flame of his exhausted lighter, hoping for a cigarette. It was time to ask for his Father's help. The discussion would be tense, that was guaranteed. Johnny did not disturb his Father for much at all, because nothing was without consequence when it came to Family—but Tora needed to get out of that hell hole. He'd been locked up at Boggo Road for over eighty days. Time was up, he felt it, cold in his bones.

Noon came and went. Johnny prepared to visit Shuji Sato, by appointment at his Cove home, where mangroves were replaced with blonde champagne, and yachts tethered to their grinning, drunken masters. There were no mosquitos there anymore, and nobody thought about it.

The house was an immense block of blue glass and stainless steel rigging—a wedge of shine that sliced its space on the crescent and overhung the canal with authority.

Italian marble dolphins danced upon their tails and rolling metallic spheres, under a spray of crystalline water. Blinding white river stones bridged the expanse between an amphitheatre of turf and the front entrance of the house. Johnny parked the Beast on the street, she leaked oil, and last time that happened Johnny had to turn the dozens of stained white orbs over to conceal the damage before his Father noticed.

Johnny stood tall and correct when announcing his arrival with a deliberate push of the electronic doorbell. He had already been cleared by security at the Cove Estate entrance, and it was these formalities he despised most. The security guards were clearly disgruntled by Johnny's car and his appearance, within the freshly walled estate that housed the *by invitation only* country club and lodge.

The interior of Mr Sato's home begged immaculate behaviour of its guests, especially when serious business was at hand, and especially when it was Family. Johnny had always complied, a force against his will allowed him to sail through interactions with his Father, although never attaining the perfection wished upon him.

The doors opened, and he removed his boots. *I probably should have left them at the front gate with the car, and be done with it.* Johnny knew how he was read under this roof. Boots quickly say too much about a man, and in Mr Sato's house, boots such as these were a sign of the wrong kind of work. Johnny reframed his thoughts, reminding himself he was here for Tora, and to Mr Sato,

Tora was a man of honour. Johnny found this more amusing than alarming and recalled that his Father had never seen Tora in shoes at all. Needless to say, in the following hours, Mr Sato had organised Tora's legal affairs and dismissed his son from the blue glassed wedge of shine with a flat-lined smile.

$$\sim$$

The heavy drapes of the afternoon closed early. La Quinta's cloud coloured diving board was gripped at the edge of the pool by bolts bleeding rust on the archaic iron frame. Ash's legs hung over the side, with her pallid bare feet breaking the view of the stagnated tropical broth that collected beneath her, in the deep end, like an old soup spoon. Ash wondered if people had deep-ends too. A swirling broth of unanswered questions from the collective unconsciousness formed. Unrequited love that went back into the ages, anguish, hope, a million kisses, a thousand deaths preserved in our DNA; all with eternal chanting from monks who drowned in the sea of Samsara —*Better luck next time,* they'd cry.

Ash's ammunition of pebbles, like rotten teeth, were shot at her distant chalked mural on the face of the swimming pool's blanched concrete. The shallow end was stained with frangipanis and hibiscus, baked into the cavernous shell over the past two months since Jay drained it, on the eve of her twenty-first birthday. She was certain people had shallow ends, half empty with sunstroked reflections of futility.

The backdrop of La Quinta, with her rolled shoulders and darkening windows, made her look less like a wedding cake, and more like a fretting bride, veiled by the baked ivy that clung to her crusted skin in a web of scars. Her paint bubbled and peeled, like a skin of boiled milk.

Upon the rooftop, Nebraska crouched at its highest peak, an immaculate gargoyle scanning the horizon for predators and lovers. Her regal form hunched under the nauseous sky, her chin pointing to Ash from beneath a shroud of rusty hair. She was surrounded by a coven of crows, and envy passed through Ash, for it was sure Nebraska could understand their every song. The birds chorused, and Nebraska tapped a beat on the rooftop with a flat hand, without a sound.

'Ice will rain, he comes down in thunder, flee with the dogs,' Ash heard.

The screen door squealed and slammed, announcing Jay to the stage, forcing Ash to take her eyes off the convulsing sky.

'I'm goin'out front. It's pumping. Make me somethin' while I'm out.'
'Uh huh. Chips?'
'Yeah, whatever. What ya doin'?'
'Just taking a look at some flowers that blew in... there's a storm coming.'

Jay left the yard, and Nebraska went like the crows. Ash cast her last pebble while studying the chalked mural of longing, before taking her layers of brooding upstairs.

The glow from outside brought a certain luminance to the swirling aquamarine hall. Ash followed the buttery yellow pools of light to Tora's door, carrying a cup of water for the, by now, parched bonsai. He had left everything behind, including his spirit, for Ash to gently hold when she was gifted small solitudes.

The white bed, under the oversized front window, beckoned her with every passing. Today she couldn't resist, and bit her lip in anticipation as she dared lay on his cool sheets for the very first time. His scent was gone, but resting her head on his pillow was enough. The caress of everything immersed her into a lull of euphoria. She gently rolled her hips side to side, inspecting the view from his pillow, this way and that. The daylight, a dulling nectar, poured in and over her skin.

If only Tora knew what La Quinta had become since he was dragged to prison. During the past eighty-eight days, the house had become a jungle, as Jay's garden had expanded exponentially, filling the garage with green lines of potted marijuana plants. At every turn of the house, they seemed to be leering, groping in the halls like Triffids, budding furiously under the adoring eye of their keeper. The same could be told of the cash now stored in all Nanna's best hiding spots; the freezer, the flour-tin, the hems of drapes, the broken ceiling vent in the bathroom. *Make every dollar your captive,* Jay had started preaching, as if he was keeper of financial secrets for some used car salesman.

Tora's bedroom, the sanctuary, was the last place in the house not to be greened by Jay and the boys who were unconscious passengers on his bandwagon.

The silver wallpaper now enveloped the room a darker shade, as the light mellowed and surrendered to the gathering clouds. Ash turned to change view. Now she could see the wardrobe door ajar, the break in-between the maplewood panels may as well have been a doorway into another dimension, luring her. It struck Ash that she could afford to take a quick peek inside, just to feel closer to Tora, feeding her desire and curiosity. Before Ash could stop herself, she was opening the door, and her hand was in the proverbial cookie jar.

It was sparsely stocked, not much clothing, some ski-looking boots, snowboard, a baseball bat. Top shelf; some vinyl stacked high, a crocheted blanket in duck egg blue that looked like it would smell of baby powder, plus one dusty shoebox, *Reebok-11-Black. One dusty shoebox*, Ash whispered as if there were now two accomplices in this tiny heist.

The sky released its first rumble, as it heaved green. The shoebox was plunged into the carpet, timed with her bare knees crashing into the softness. Ash held her hands over the box ceremoniously before lifting the lid with hungry pink claws. She was excited, the box was heavier than shoes and rattled. This was treasure.

The lid was cast aside, and its contents exposed—two well-thumbed novels: *Homer's Odyssey* (hence the weight), and *Nineteen Eighty-Four* (lightweight but packed a punch). Ash gently tipped the loot onto the carpet and spread the items out. The books were inscribed to Tora from his Father, The *Odyssey* in 1977, and *Nineteen Eight-Four* in 1984. Ash wished she hadn't touched them, putting them back in the box carefully.

Onto smaller things, knick-knacks that Ash would never understand the significance of, and a couple of items that did directly relate to her—precisely what she wanted to find. A Polaroid of her with Ninja, taken in the kitchen after the Nirvana concert and a heart-shaped box the colour of garnet. Ash prized it open like a clam. A ring in the form of a mermaid, with a glistening tail twisted delicately around the circumference, to meet waves of hair. Inside the ring, engraved like a tattoo on her golden back, *Ash & Tora 1991*.

A salty sting flushed her eyes, there was more; a mixtape called *Driving home: Oceans, Patience, All of My Love, The Witch, The Real Thing, Crimson and Clover, One More night... Phil Collins? What?* Ash started laughing. She was smiling, and crying, what a raw feeling. With that, Ash claimed the ring, sliding it on her finger giving a jolt of energy from the Gods. The sky roared with a yearning that she felt in her heart, a yearning for immediate change, decisive action. Strength had arrived, and she was saying *Yes—Now*, to her neglected self. It was time to leave. Ash remembered, in her Mother's voice, '*You were born in a storm, a storm that inundated the city.*' A great storm was bearing down on La Quinta now, and Ash knew she could simply run!

She burst into the yellow wall-papered bedroom and tore her waiting bag from under the bed, along with her repurposed Tupperware *firebox*. She slid into her thongs and climbed out onto the roof, the air smelled of hail—cold like an open freezer, and she scrambled down the ladder. With her bag swinging and a thumping heart, she traced the lichen speckled fenceline to the curb. She turned west on Monaco Street, into the jowls of the brewing storm, avoiding the path of Jay, who was east in the treacherous sea a few blocks away. Zoe's place was less than ten blocks, she could make it if she bolted—before the sky raged upon the sun-worshipping city.

And just like that, she was out.

CHAPTER SEVENTEEN

Riders Of The Storm

A shrill ruptured the sky, and with the strike of its mistress, the Coast was silenced and cowered to the sea. Monaco Street was an eerie shade of both light and dark, and the cars parked like army worms huddled for their execution. La Quinta quivered as the boys crowded her trembling foyer, wet dogs on thin shanks. They'd made it home, but Oli had lost his board to the jaws of the sea. That never happened, it was an exceptional afternoon. They scampered to their rooms leaving wet footprints to seep into the dim halls, with Moose in hurried pursuit of his next hiding spot.

'Ash! Where's my food? I'm starvin'.'

Jay paced the aquamarine pile ominously, his dripping wetsuit pulled low and swinging, like drooling serpents from his surf-bruised hips. His eyes searched for shadows and imprints of her.

'Ash? Where are ya?'

Nothing but thunder answered. Jay stopped at Tora's threshold. The room aglow with a murky atmosphere, an iron lung with brooding pewter walls. The only sign of life was the all-knowing bonsai. The mysteries, the truths, the afterlife, Eternal Dreaming, Valhalla, Shambhala, Merkaba, Heaven, Hell, all that was before and all that will be; lay dormant in its quenched roots, a sleeping mystic. Beside it, a near-empty beer bottle and water pooled lucid at its feet.

Jay's nostrils flared, eyes pink from sea lashings, he took a white-knuckled grip and ripped the tree from its antique pot. Soiled water bled into the sandy carpet as he held the tiny mammoth by its trunk. He kicked open his bedroom door, wide enough to reveal its vacancy. The wind swirled, the drapes snapped, taught and bleak, as they tacked headlong into the storm. Ash was gone. He cried her name, over and over, into the deafness, punching the ribbed wallpaper until it bled dust.

Thunder and lightning arced, with tremors and stabs of virgin white, filling the yards of canal dollhouses in shuddering intermissions. Then, all could hear galloping upon them, thunderously, boldly and violently, without avoidance. In shards, golf balls, cricket balls, blocks of ice like old freezers shaken empty. Shot guns and wild horses, a stampede of hail stormed the house.

Then, the most terrific crash of all. The bedroom was opened like a yolk. An enormous *widow maker* limb had prized itself through the ceiling with a wash of rainwater, onto the crooked single bed. A deluge rushed into the house with small branches gently stabbing Jay's bare torso, inverted with fear. Jay watched as his room filled with a cocktail of leaves, limbs, insects, water and ice. He backed against the broken wall, astonished by this force larger than he, drunken with power, nature had taken all its fury and expressed it with proper conviction. Jay understood perfectly.

He left the room, stepping over broken glass that sheeted the aquamarine hall, swirling with milky water and ripped leaves. The rain blew in, and the hail passed. Sirens were calling in tandem on the distant littered streets, whilst block after block was ripped off the grid with callous rage. The plastic sheeting of the front window (that Jay had thrown the chair through), had broken free and wrapped around a buckling palm, flowing like a faded gymnast's ribbon in the bluster.

Downstairs seemed intact. The power was out, and tremors of thunder rattled the windows. Oli, Racer, Skinny and Jay stood dumbfounded in the lounge room like defeated superheroes. Another crash. The boys bounded upstairs to see what was to come. Jay's bedroom ceiling had caved in. Ash's cage was crushed. The bedroom was gone, except Jay's nursery, which sat in the wardrobe unscathed and happy for the rain. La Quinta was finished, a violent death had been bestowed upon her. To Jay, she had been stabbed in the heart with one fatal blow, just as he. Ash had fled the storm like a fearful dog—Jay had already justified her actions. Tomorrow he'd bring her home, and they'd start over *his way*.

Another crash. Again, the boys raced to see what was to come. They were met at the staircase by two men in balaclavas, each clasping a glistening weapon with a belly full of bullets. The sky clapped loud, and lightning flashed, announcing the start of the show.

'Where do ya' think ya' goin'?' one asked the wet, trembling wolves. 'We're here to blow ya fuckin' house down!' he closed off with a roar of laughter, insanely.

'What the fuck do ya want?' Jay yelled.

Oli and Skinny, slack-jawed, hit the deck. Racer didn't move a muscle, he couldn't have spoken if he tried. The boys had never seen real guns before. Jay had, when James took him to a friend's place down at Crystal Creek to *'Pick something up for a mate'*.

'Shut the fuck up Jay-Jay. You boys are gonna sit at that table before I blow your tops off! Move now!' he commanded. 'Where's yah girl Jay-Jay?'

'Not 'ere.'

'Well then, you're 'avin a rough time aren't ya? I don't bloody blame 'er, ya soft cock. Ha ha!'

Out came the rope, and out went Jay's garden. Each and every plant was marched into a panel-van under the silent shroud of the storm. The cash too... Jay was stunned they knew all the hiding places. *'Fucking Ash must'a told'em,'* he cursed.

The day surrendered to night and rain hammered the withering rooftop. The boys sat around the table in their habitual seats with their hands and feet tied. All they had to look at was each other's unprepared boyish faces, drawn and slack. When they closed their eyes, they smelled the open wounds of the house, her walls buckled and seeped as she was gutted.

'Finally got my fifty bucks back, ya asshole. If you fucking move a muscle before dawn, we'll fuckin' finish yah all!'

And just like that, the garden, the cash and the girl were gone. One storm. Jay had the night to ponder his loss, his defeat and his future, as he pulled away at the frayed rope until his raw burning wrists were freed. The boys were tied, sleeping on their chairs, with nowhere much better to be. At dawn, they obediently and wordlessly returned to their quarters to lick their wounds, and pack for their next move, except for Jay.

Jay wandered onto the front yard and looked at dawns' freshly minted sky, awash with clean sunshine. He turned his nose to the breeze as if to catch a scent. By deduction, Jay decided to pay a visit to Zoe. He knew where she lived, he tried so hard to fuck her last year, and that bitch kept refusing him. *She's probably a starfish anyway*, he sneered as he tightened his grip on the wilted bonsai, its body losing colour in whispered shades of grey, its forlorn leaves bowing to the soaked earth.

It was a long ten blocks back to La Quinta. One hand white, gloved inside Jay's grip and the other, forced to carry the tiny mammoth's carcass home. Tears rolled numbly down Ash's neck, slowing at the shallow rise of breath. Ash's cotton bag swung, empty, with her fern green *firebox* left behind.

They had no bedroom to speak of. The only proper shelter remaining was Tora's bedroom. Jay carried Ash over broken glass that paved the hall, and then over the threshold. He dropped her hard onto Tora's bed, polluting the room with his sombre presence, thick as tar.

'You're here with me now, baby. Just the two of us. The boys are leaving and it's gonna be my way from here. Understand?' he clasped her chin, then squeezed harder. 'Yes?'
'Yes,' and rolled to face the wall, the bonsai dry in her limp red hand.

Jay left the room, and Ash didn't move until she heard him return with a soft clank on the wall. He held a black metal bar, raised it high and then dropped a sharp end into the damp carpet with clout. She didn't flinch. She felt the circumference of that ring grip her finger, and she didn't flinch. She'd been outside now. She'd felt her thumping heart fill her chest as she ran, the invigoration, the fear lifting her high above her centre, she'd tasted freedom—all the way to the edges.

'You might wanna find the cat. I haven't seen 'er since the storm,' he said, low.

Jay dragged the bar across the floor as he approached, grabbed her hair and kissed her forehead with strange intensity. He left the room again and didn't return for the longest time. She grew hungry, and the light escaped without remedy. Curled on limp sheets, Ash waited like an animal for her keeper in the blue dark. She watched the silver wallpaper turn its shades with a picture show of reflections and shadows that melted and evolved, until they became swirling memories in her jilted sleep.

It felt like midnight when Jay lay beside her with a tight embrace. Her frozen limbs gave nothing back to his pressing hips. He breathed warmly into her knotted locks, promising he would never let her go, never ever. Blow by blow, the night was long, the longest she had lived since that first Monday of July, and her skin took on the shades of the wallpaper that embraced the room. Metallic and still, she rode the hours.

Dawn came back, and the birds sang as they always had. They didn't know what had happened inside. They weren't to blame. Ash tread the aquamarine hall to go to the bathroom, to find some food, and find Ninja. The boys' voices were echoing in the hollowed house, now mostly dust and bones.

'Tora's gettin' out any day now.' Racer announced.
'Yeah, as if. Who told ya?' Jay asked.
'Johnny was out front.'
'Too bad we're evicted ay? We got two days,' Oli spoke up. 'I guess we're no good 'ere without a roof. Tora's gonna be spewin'... me, Racer'n Skinny are leavin' today. I'm gonna go back to Dee Why ay... Fuck this place.'
'Ash and I are leavin' tomorrow. Yeah, Tora's

gonna come back to zero, fucking nothin'.'

'Where ya goin?'

'More south. Best waves, ay?'

'How far?'

'Far enough. It's no good for Ash up 'ere near Surfers.'

Ash sat on the top step of the stairs that twisted and turned like the inside of a dead snail shell. She was weakened by everything, by the light, by needing to breathe, by having to see. Her senses hurt, her eyes burned, she could feel bruises pulsing on her face from the omnipresent night. The skin of her body felt crisp as rice paper that would tear at the slightest tension, and that she filled it, unwillingly, to its brim. Translucent and pulsing with pain over a web of bones, she pulled fingers of hair forward, covering her silver jaw, panda eye and swollen cherry mouth. Ash's face fell to her knees in surrender.

'He'll never love you like he does me.' Nebraska whispered as if others may hear, and leaned with levity over the balustrade, high on her translucent toes. 'Never ever,' she chanted before her decadent smile faded in naked ripples, and her dull eyes fell.

Ash saw solstice in the revenant's face now. The wintery storm had torn at her, wantonly and unforgiving, and La Quinta, Nebraska's catafalque, battered and poised for abandonment. Soon, she feared, she'd be alone.

CHAPTER EIGHTEEN

Mr Damage

A brine-washed breeze combed the Monaco Street palm trees. The storm debris had been cleared, and the pitted cars were last of the evidence. Jay stood outside, leaning with his tobacco brown torso, with a predator's posture, as he inspected his car. One hand ran over his matt of salt waxed hair, and the other reached out to walk fingers over the purple metallic paint. *The damage wasn't too bad.*

Ash sat on Tora's ruined bed and scanned the room as if to say the last goodbye. The horrors of this house would never shadow the love she'd felt for him within those walls and the hope he'd given her; she at least promised herself that. Jellybean yellow caught her eye, pulsing like outrageous sunshine, those skateboard wheels were enough to light the room. She finally wanted to give it a try and had been waiting for an opportunity to ride the skull of La Quinta's pool ever since Jay drained it. It was now or never. Ash felt assured by now that Tora wouldn't mind, he did offer after all. As for Jay, he *would* care, but may not realise since he's so busy with other things. She permitted herself to take the skateboard and wandered into the broken yard.

Nebraska basked in the sun, belly-up, on the diving board. Her hair awash with white light, she swung her limbs aimlessly over the stagnant broth as she sang *'It's never too late,'* to the sky. Ash sealed her red eyes and meditatively took a deep breath, all the way to the bottom of her lungs, thinking of Edie on exhale. She positioned the skateboard on the swimming pool rim and dropped into the steep grey curve. Ash was exhilarated as she pushed into the air, untouchable. The skateboard slowed, skimming the deep end that was black as a cauldron, peppered with blossoms, faded and bewildered. The yellow wheels halted with a march of pebbles underfoot.

Ash sat on the warm concrete and appreciated the breeze wrapping her narrowed shoulders while she studied her mural of half-washed chalk beneath the eroded steps. Built with childlike swirls of rainbow flaked dust, it now read *bla k ridg*. Ash knew that no matter how many times she clicked her cracked bare heels, there'd be no way home. She had lost her mind, courage and heart. When she rose, the skateboard rolled to the lip of the dark broth, its wheels dusted with broken rainbows. She abandoned the skateboard and left the pool behind, it'd been a hell of a ride.

Jay was ready for the getaway. Ash stood in the long

grass and mauvish weeds, holding Ninja tight to her breast, protective as a nursing Mother. Her cotton bag hung listlessly over her shoulder, weightless, for she had nothing left. At a distance, a fresh sound pulsed the ground and vibrated to the curb—through to her bare feet. The noise grew familiar as it drew near, that rumbling, that growling engine. Ash felt the blood drain from her face, her legs suddenly no stronger than wilted reeds.

From behind, the Beast pulled up with all eight cylinders breathing down the neck of Jay's car. Johnny killed his engine, announcing the longest silence. All had stopped. The passenger door opened, and the stainless steel trim grabbed the sun. Tora emerged from the black car without lightness, dark and lean. His eyes blanked and fixed on Ash, with tender resolve. Ash took a step back in reflex, with trained anxiety. Tora shifted his focus from her eyes to *all of her*. Pale, thin, in a torn dress, coloured with grazes and bruises, her mouth a flaming sunset, smacked with pain. He saw his ring on her porcelain finger as she buried her hands into the cat's inky fur with a tremble. She couldn't look at him, there was no way she could let him in.

Jay locked his stare with a clenched jaw, not willing to speak, not this time.

'What's going on?' Tora asked, balancing the shudder of his voice.
'We gotta get out.'
'Why?'

'The house got trashed. You weren't 'ere to deal with it.'

'Where ya going?' Tora bowed his head to the weed knotted grass.

'We're moving.'

'Where?'

'Fuck you.'

Jay got into his car. Tora gave Ash a look of urgency and appeal, they locked eyes for a devastating and luxuriant moment. Ash backed towards the car and fumbled the door. Tora stepped forward to help before he stopped himself. She blindly crawled into the passenger seat, pregnant with fear and desire. The car pulled away with a jolt as Ash watched Tora watch her, in the broken mirror as she disappeared.

Tora had never felt so wounded, like a Toro Bravo overcome with a hundred banderillas plunged into his withers. He entered the foyer of his home, although he could've stepped straight through the missing front window that exposed the house to the elements.

Climbing the stairs, he treaded the hall that whispered underfoot. The broken glass refracted the sun to the stained walls in pools of flickering light and guided him to the end—to Jay's bedroom. He pushed the door open and saw nothing and everything. The crooked single bed appeared asleep under the crushing weight of the fallen grey limb, and a flurry of nature had assailed past the torn curtains, now more outside than in. The wardrobe gutted, the posters torn, and the only thing that remained intact was the punched holes Jay left with calculated precision next to the doorframe. Tora turned and stumbled into his own room wanting to collapse where the bonsai pot lay in mud and broken bones, on the spongey wet carpet.

His room held his possessions, still, but an element unthinkable to replace was missing—the ambience of *her*. He went to the window to look over the war-torn front yard, littered with the neighbourhood's garden offcuts and broken dreams of boyhood, rusted and decrepit. There was one thing that struck him as odd; a matchbook from The Cheshire Cat Motel left on the window sill. He opened it. Two matches left, side by side.

'Where'd they go?' Johnny broke the void.
'7th Ave. Palmy.'

They paced the weeping hall. Tora with his surfboard under his arm and a polaroid of Ash at his hip. He stopped to look out to the swimming pool. His skateboard rested on the parched concrete, and finally, Tora half-smiled.

He and Johnny crossed the loungeroom, passing Nebraska, face down on the couch, limp limbed, translucent, invisible. Her cries were soundless as she mourned the dwelling that had magnetised her spirit, and he who drew her there.

The Beast rumbled along the coast highway, catching every red light between Surfers and Palm Beach, making for a slow advance. Glimpses of blue horizon winked brightly as they passed oceanside avenues, one block after the next.

'He leaves a path of destruction,' Tora was exasperated now that the shock had passed. 'Ten years I've leased that place. I'm locked up a few months, and now I'm out. I come back to nothing. I could've been left to rot with all the shit they found. I know it was Jay, but I can't believe he would have done that to me,' he finally exhaled. 'I owe your Dad man, thanks again Johnny.'

Johnny simply nodded and pulled up outside The Cheshire Cat Motel.

'I'll swing by after rehearsal?' Johnny suggested.
'Yeah man, see ya later.' Tora shut the heaving black door with his foot, carrying his board and a small bag of clothes.

Tora took in the Palm Beach neighbourhood and wondered how the motel played a part in this tragedy. The highway traffic subsided, and Tora's eye was drawn to the caravan park across the way. *Golden Sands Caravan Park $9 O'nite*, the tired sign smiled. Beyond a gap-toothed hibiscus hedge, Jay's purple car rested, and an askew caravan with its blinds pulled tight, huddled beside like a tin box tethered to the sandy earth.

Tora found it hard to turn away from the caravan site as he walked toward the motel reception office. The doorbell rang with a startle when he entered the dusty office. Behind the tall lacquered counter, a ball of bleached, pasta coloured hair sprung beyond its horizon, followed by chirpy blue eyes and a full cheeked smile. The receptionist perched behind her Olivetti typewriter, a few telephones and the backdrop, a proud rack of room keys. She eventually peered high over the partition to greet Tora.

'Hello Darl.'

'G'day, I'd like a room for tonight. Facing the street, if you can?'

'Ok, let's see... Yes! Room two will be perfect for you. Its got a spa bath and a compact disc player. Our honeymooners love it. It's thirty-eight dollars. Per night.' Scrunching her nose, anxious for a decision.

'I don't think I'll get time to use the spa, but that room sounds great, thanks,' he smiled.

Tora observed the office while waiting for the receptionist to do her thing. Forever. Looking through the smudged door, he saw Jay leaning against his car outside the old caravan, smoking the last of a cigarette before flicking the butt to the sand and going inside.

Room two was airless and had a broad windowed front that faced the west. It sent crushing heat through the metallic Venetian blinds that weaved golden light into the long-locked room of lovers. Under the window was a table for two, with a centrepiece of dusty plastic roses that embraced in a dry vase. An elaborate glass ashtray sat beside, longing for fire. The chairs, lime vinyl with ninety-degree efficiency, seemed to be spared from the reception office downstairs. Tora sat rigidly, reaching his full span to open the window wide, letting in the sea air, and perfect view of Jay's caravan which crouched in the sand, tight as a clam. Tora waited to see a glimpse of her. Her alone.

The hum of traffic penetrated the caravan's paper-thin walls, and the heat punched in through the cracked open windows. Steam danced and recoiled from a small saucepan when Ash served instant noodles into a pair of orange plastic bowls. Jay sat at the small table hugged by a scratchy polyester booth, waiting to be served.

'Watch out, it's super hot.' Ash warned as she carefully landed the bowls.

'They look shit. How is it that ya' fuck up even the most simple things?'

Jay whacked the bowl of boiling noodles, and they flung across the tiny enclosure of the caravan. Ash jumped to her feet to escape the lava and backed away.

'How much stupidity do you think I can take? Huh? How much!'

Jay grabbed his cigarettes from the bedside. Ninja was resting on the bed curled on top of Ash's bag. Jay lit a cigarette and took a deep drag. He stared at its glowing end, then at Ash, and exhaled his dark cloud. Paralysed with fear, Ash glanced at the locked caravan door and wondered if bolting was worth a shot. Her thought was breathlessly overtaken when Jay picked up Ninja by her scruff and held the cigarette too close to her exposed face.

'You wanna see what happens when I've had enough? Do you? Answer me!'

'No. Please put her down. I'll make something else.'

Jay threw the kitten back down onto the bed with measured force. He walked towards Ash rocking the van with each heavy step, taking another drag of his cigarette as he closed in. Jay grabbed her throat and held his burning cigarette close to her skin.

'You know what I think Ash? I think you wish I was dead, so you can be with Tora. As dead as ya sista!'

'No. Jay. Baby. That's not true,' she gasped.

'Look at me. Look into my eyes. Look! You know what pain is Ash? Do ya know how much pain you've brought me?'

Jay took the burning cigarette away from Ash's face and without hesitation, put it to his neck, branding himself with his own rage.

'Argghh!'

'No! Jay! Please stop! Just stop!'

Ash grabbed Jay's arm to stop him. He released his grip with a push back onto the kitchen stove.

'I don't know how much more of this I can take!' Jay yelled.

Under Tora's constant gaze from his anonymous motel window, Jay flung the caravan door wide open, revealing Ash—who stood back and wiped her red face. Jay launched forward, reached for a discarded brick and threw it full force at his hail bitten car. One side of the windscreen ruined.

'Who's next?' he screamed to the passing cars nearby. He spun back to face Ash. 'One foot out of the van and you're fucking dead!'

Jay picked up his surfboard and waxed it harshly on the sandy ground. Ash watched nervously, standing on the doorstep, compulsively turning the golden mermaid on her finger as Jay prepared to leave. Jay marched his board over the road, through the hesitant traffic and raced toward the sea.

Tora watched over Ash who had backed into her enclosure and obediently closed the door behind her. From above, Tora saw Johnny was back in the neighbourhood, with perfect timing, true to form. His black spidery legs carried him toward the motel reception. Tora took off his shirt, grabbed his board and left, breathless.

Jay saw the Beast parked quietly on 6th Ave. He looked around, sharp as a crow, and approached the black steel body. Jay reached for his pocket knife and slid under the warm car. He bladed and sliced here and there, making as much blind damage as possible in sixty seconds, and after, wiped the grease and leaked fluid on his chest before continuing on his way. *I hate that fucking gook, and what the fuck is 'e doing 'ere*, he seethed.

Tora intercepted Johnny in the breeze block stairwell and pushed the room key into his elegant, string picking hand. 'Ash is over in that piece of shit caravan up front. Ask her to come here? Jay's gone out front. I'll keep him entertained.'

Tora was all adrenalin and he continued to bound down the stairs, in full flight.

Ash sat in a pool of hot orange burn on the threadbare polyester seat that crackled and stretched as she shifted her posture. The caravan seemed like hell to her. *'A fresh kind of hell,'* Edie would've gleefully quoted in her best Hollywood voice, to get a smile out of Ash's sullen face—when life's seasons would turn unfavourably, but it had never been like this. Ash weighed up her situation with a callous tone. She knew she would rather be killed running from this infested hot box than be killed like an exhausted, trapped animal.

The traffic seemed louder now, and a coven of crows descended in a haze of cries. *Tap, tap, tap*, came from the roof, silent to all but Ash. She stood with resigned breath, palms pressed flat on the filthy chipboard table, as the dreadful daylight fell all around. Ash missed her Mother. She wanted to go home. She harboured the urge to run, run all the way home. Ninja was scooped up by Ash and delicately kissed goodbye. It was time to set her free.

There stood Johnny at the open caravan door, statuesque and grinning in the brightness of the afternoon.

'Hi. Ah.' Briefly distracted by her necklace. 'Tora is staying over the road in room two,' he casually pointed behind him. 'Don't come back here,' he said while swinging the room key in-between them.

Ash handed Ninja to Johnny in exchange for the motel key and cautiously stepped out into the open air.

Johnny stood in the caravan and peered out of the murky kitchen window where noodles clung to the fly screen like maggots. He snarled with humour, then squinted as he lit a cigarette on the gas cooker's blue flame. Johnny observed Ninja as she trotted past the caravan before he looked around to survey its contents.

He stepped out of the caravan and casually walked away with a surge of satisfaction rising in his chest. Three, two, one... he breathed in a *Whoosh!* Within moments the caravan was a ball of flames, licked visciously from the inside by red heat and yellow tallons of fire. Johnny never looked back.

Tora arrived at the shoreline as a man going into battle, he studied the waves and pounced the curling water, feline. With absolute prowess, he paddled out swiftly and waited. He tailed Jay as he paddled for a wave and then squarely dropped in on him.

Tora and Jay were side by side out front of 7th Ave, encircled by a pack of locals.

'Why are you doing this?' Tora was calm.

'We're doing great.'

'We?'

'Yeah. Me'n Ash.'

'She's not and you know it.'

'Fuck you Tora, always thinking you know shit.'

'I know you!'

Jay launched at Tora, grabbed his board and punched him. Tora made little effort to avoid the swing. Jay's punch was answered with Tora tipping Jay off his surf board like a child. Jay, furious, scrambled back onto his board and pulled out his knife.

'Don't be scared to walk alone... my little brother,' Tora cooed.

'Fuck you. You're nothin to me! Burn in hell Tora.'

'Let her go,' he demanded.

Jay raised his knife and Tora responded by swiftly knocking it into the sea. It sank into the blue, just as Jay wished he could. He had nothing left out in the water, he was defenceless and left the darkening sea.

A billow of smoke hovered darkly above the reddening west and the horizon of flat-roofed motels. From the rim of the restless highway, and creeping headlights, Jay saw his caravan ablaze. Ash was gone, again! He torpedoed his grease printed surfboard to the ground and pushed his pointed face to the sky, yelling in vain to the muffled concrete landscape.

Room two was dim. The blinds were pinched closed with a second layer of drapes. Fluorescent light bled in from the top, but not enough to take away from the bedside lamp, red with desire, as it looked to the disused bed, and the girl sitting barely on its edge in a shock of emotion. Ash had nothing left but was grateful to have everything. This too, would pass, and she would survive.

The door opened slowly to Tora's wet figure. He moved towards Ash ever so tentatively, knelt down and collected her face with his eyes, taking in all he could. He saw the world in her eyes and wiped a tear from her blue cheek and kissed it. Their hands tightly clutched, rested on her thighs, and he fixed his gaze low. The golden ring was luminous in a slither of light that pushed in from the motel sign outside.

'I can't feel much anymore,' she whispered.
'It's over now. I'll get you outta here.'
'I created all of this. I waited so long, too long...
I thought you'd just walk in one day and... then I was trapped. The more I struggled the harder it got. I thought... we'd be together. I'm sorry. And now it all seems too late... so damaged,' Ash confided.
'We were together Ash. Every day, every night. Don't ever think it was for nothing. I felt you. No more waiting,' he touched her hair.

Ash stood and released her velvet grip of his hand. She turned the mermaid once, twice on her finger.

Dusk settled pink on the horizon to applaud the rising

full moon that glimmered over the strident sea. Jay stared at the Cheshire Cat Motel from the street like a ghost, as headlights streamed behind him. He broke the night with calls for her.

'I know you're here Ash! Come out and see me baby!'

Ash softly pulled away from Tora and moved to look out the window, through the split of the drapes. She watched Jay below, standing with tangled hair, under a warm streetlight, with grease and black ash on his chest.

'I need to finish this,' Ash spoke towards the window, her voice bounced back at her.

Ash was out and slammed the honeymoon suite door behind her. She ran along the motel balcony, crazed and disoriented like a fugitive. Tora followed her closely and stopped short halfway when Ash turned back and signalled him to stop. Tora stayed where he was, his eyes were fixed on Ash before he turned to look at Jay in the car park below. Jay glared back at Tora, his eyes burning with rage. Ash marched downstairs to the car park and confronted Jay with an alien stare, cold and steel. She powerfully stopped inches from his face, filled with foolish rage.

'Why don't you go all the way Jay-Jay? Just do it already!' as she gripped her own throat. 'Instead of dragging me through your misery every minute of the fucking day.'

'I love you Ash,' Jay said, swallowing his words. 'Tora can't love you, not like you need. Stay with me. Please. I'm sorry.'

Tora watched a short distance away, his heart choking. Ash stepped in closer to Jay as if she would kiss him. He didn't move. He didn't know what to expect from her, she was erratic and unpredictable. She was a challenge, and he loved her more for it.

'You love nothing Jay. Nothing! You only see things. Not people. You make me sick! You make me wish I was dead! Do you hear me? Do you?'

Ash launched at him and pushed his chest with both shaking hands, venomously. She felt a surge, like a warrior fighting until her last breath, expecting to be struck at any moment by his tumultuousness.

Tora slowly moved closer to Ash, and Jay stood motionless. Without her internal warning systems preparing her, Ash swung at Jay and hit his face. He looked to Tora, his once caring guardian now pacing toward him like a raging dog.

Jay raised a hand to strike Ash, hesitated and took a few steps back. He turned and walked away—back to the charred carcass of his new home.

Ash wasn't done. 'C'mon Jay-Jay. C'mon *baby!*' she cried with a vengeance through her tears. 'You will never see me again! Never ever!'

Tora held her, and she pulled away with a thundering growl. She ran, stopping at the curb for a moment, then bolted. Tora gave chase, and Ash ran even faster.

'Leave me... just leave me. I'm not here to be saved. You can't tag me like a bird, it's not gonna fix anything,' Ash cried over her shoulder. She tossed the ring onto the prickled sidewalk, in total abandonment—of everything.

'You never gave me a chance to tell you Ash, to ask you...' he called.

'Nobody can hold me anymore,' and she burst into a tearful sprint.

Soon her words would crush under his feet with every step, as he walked through the memories of that day.

No beginning, no end.

CHAPTER NINETEEN

Cat's In The Cradle

The taxi interior glowed warm with sobering intimacy, fumes fell heavy and mean from the exhaust, and the driver, large in his seat, seemed all shoulders and neck from behind, like a bulldog stuffed in a tight shirt.

'Monaco Street, Surfers Paradise please mate,' James asked.

His hand pressed on the tan leather suitcase that rested on his lap. It looked creased and scuffed, perhaps from too many taxi rides like this. There were two in the set originally, but Moreen took a shine to the bigger one and stuffed it full of her shoes. Before she left. Last Tuesday. That was the end of his second suitcase.

'It's going to be about fifteen bucks to get up there. Okay mate?'
'Let me check... Yeah it'll be right.'
'What number?'
'1991.'

James felt childlike as he rode in the back seat, knowing he had nowhere to be and had just a single chance of being taken in. His new boots were stiff like an old man's back, and their barely scratched soles rubbed the freshly vacuumed floor mats. His attention drifted to the blur of nights' pavements and pillars that blew past under the shadows of nothing. It was a long way, Palm Beach to Surfers Paradise when circumstances weren't the best.

La Quinta was darker than James ever remembered, with dead vines clinging to every extremity, curling away at the roofline like a straw hat. James got out of the cab with his suitcase and a cough. He was aware of his stillness, and the raw sight of him ragged and shod with painful new shoes. His old possessions were crushed into that suitcase which he'd been given in Nerang that time the Salvo's picked him up. He confronted the abandoned house with a stone face and walked across the unkempt lawn towards the entrance.

Knock. Knock. Knock,

'Hello? Jay, it's me, Dad,' cough. 'Are you home?'

The doorbell was dead. James moved across to the broken front window that had tangles of tape and plastic hanging from the corners and climbed in. James didn't know the house well enough to walk around in the dimness and just waited a while. He was not prepared for this. The house made noises all her own but nobody was home, and nobody was coming back.

The irony of it all was too much to bear.

Nebraska lay on the damp couch with her closed face cushioned on the velvet between a plastic rubbish bag stuffed with old clothes and some tools Racer left behind from the shaping bay.

'Jay, I've been waiting,' she smiled into the pressed fabric with futility, knowing full well he would never hear her, never ever.

'Darlin' shouldn't you get some clothes on?' James voice cracked in the half light.

Nebraska stood elegantly from the couch and stepped forward with precision, celestial, in her crown of auburn.

'He sees me.'
'Yes. Maybe more than I'm supposed to.'
'And he hears me.'
'Where's Jay?' James asks anxiously.
'You don't know who I am?'
'No, sorry darlin' I wish I did though,' he laughed and trailed off as he immediately felt inappropriate.
'He never took me to meet his Father. That always hurt. I guess I said *no* the first time... but he could have tried again. Why are guys like that?'
'Jay?'
'I'm the Other One. We were to be married.'
'Oh. I see. But now? There's Ash...'
'No, she ran.'
'Oh. You kids are complicated. I'm an old man. I'm

sick. Darling, please put on some clothes.'

'You'll get used to it. This is how he left me, so this is how I must stay.'

'Oh. I won't get used to it, it's very distracting. You stay naked, but I'm gonna try not to look at you, with all my God-given strength. Nothin but trouble...' James drifted.

He crouched to the floor and flipped his suitcase flat, releasing the rusted clasps—they sprung open. He held up a pressed formal shirt. It was pink and his very best.

'Here. This'll fit.'

'You will take me to him,' she said wistfully. 'A man's feet are responsible for him; they lead him to the place where he is wanted.'

'*Please*, just put this on,' James sighed.

Nebraska reached out and showed that her hand went straight through the shirt like candlelight. James gaped at the sight and sat low on the floor. He put his hands to his face and sobbed with shuddering resonance. Nebraska looked on forlorn, she missed having the feeling of tears cool her face. He was as lost as she. They walked the world without effect, invisible to most, robbed of love and identity. She knew it in his age soaked face. He was accustomed to invisibility and as a result, seemed less shocked by her presence.

James gathered himself, refolded his pink shirt, tight and square, and closed his suitcase. He stepped outside, upon his blistered heels, using La Quinta's grand old front door, and didn't turn to see if Nebraska was following. It didn't matter.

Once across the dark mauve yard, he paused at the curb and finally chose to head east, back toward the sea. *She would have answers*, he decided. The walk under the streetlights was lonely, he could feel his fever rising. James traipsed along the crooked spine of pavement as cars sped by, bobbing their yellow lights, leaving clouds of fumes that he coughed back to the street, time and time again, until he reached the park. Exhausted.

James surrendered his shoes to the park's curious birds and walked the narrowing path barefoot, dodging spiked acorns like grenades. Nebraska walked beside him, almost two hands taller, now that he didn't have shoes on. James thought he might like to rest on the sand and undergrowth of the dune trees, but found it too cold for his lungs, despite his fever, and instead chose a bench for his hungry weariness.

Nebraska was a creature of comfort and settled on the grey sand with a tiara of bronzed pine needles. Puffs of seagulls dozed at her breast as the moon climbed a ladder of stars. Her thoughts drifted, and she wondered if Black Moon Lilith had come for James or her on this night. The nefarious goddess darted overhead, weaving through the sky, howling like the wind as she swallowed the speckled suns whole.

Through the night, Nebraska never lost sight of James, who faded into shadows as he negotiated every liquid breath. She feared he would leave her behind, to commune with Lilith, before first light. Meanwhile, James expected the naked fawn would disappear at any moment. *An apparition in times of trouble*, he pondered as he stared at the beach-bright horizon.

All night long, in and out of consciousness, his breath was against the pulling tide of the moon. James could see Jay in the murky air on his knees before him, at that park bench—strong, bold and brave. His baby boy blue. James had waited all his adult life for his son to recognise him, to see him, to cherish him. All the while, Jay was waiting for the same. James felt the tripwire of destiny push into his body, and all those chances he remembered faded into whispers of regret. Forever they would stay.

∾

His feet green with wet clover, Jay climbed the squalid stairway to James' icecream coloured door. The old key had been left in the lock and the door ajar. It dragged and caught the floorboards, swollen with anonymous history. Jay pushed inside, knowing he would find abandonment.

In the void, once James' home, one of a countless many; he lay on the gritted kitchen floor and sobbed under the purple neon wash that bounced against the walls like trapped spirits. The smell of incense lingered from elsewhere as a procession of sirens swept by.

The door slammed shut with bluster, a heavy sigh tore from Jay's crimson insides, giving nothing in return.

His Father was really gone this time.

CHAPTER TWENTY

All Of My Love

Magic Mountain hunched over the Hibiscus Lantern shopping arcade, which pushed back under the girth of the cliff in a skirt of warm lights. The tall palms crowned with green tufts danced in the breeze like cheerleader pom-poms. The derelict amusement park haunted the headland, day and night. With only its ghost lights on, it was dressed for demolition. Collective memory was soon to be lost; Magic Mountain, where bright-sunned children and handsome salt n' pepper Dads would whiz down hot metal slides like unfurled tongues, on hession sacs with fairy-floss fingers their only grip.

The phone booth on Chairlift Ave resonated with nothing except the sound of Ash's hardened breath. She leaned against the interior glass, the receiver in her lowered hand beeped an expired dial tone. Her freedom felt cold to the touch as she took time to rest her bruises on the night cooled surfaces that lined the booth.

Ash pressed the receiver down to reset her path. 0—1—3.

Ring. Ring.

'Operator. How can I assist?'
'Reverse charge call please...' Ash stalled. 'Black Ridge. 7-0-7-2-6-5-0.'

A series of beeps and crackles in a wobble of noise rushed down the line. The vitals of a phone connection pushed Ash's heart to her throat. Then, a distant ring that sounded like a faraway place, in another time.

'Hello?'
'Mum it's m—' Ash's voice broke in two.
'Ash! Where are you? Where have you been honey? Henry, it's Ash!'
The operator interrupted. 'Do you accept this as a reverse charge call from the Gold Coast?'
'Yes, yes! Thank you operator,' Joan Smith had to sit down.
'Mama, can I come home? I'm sorry. I thought I could be on my own and find a life without Edie that would of made me happy. You know? Happiness for her, like she would have done for me... I'm on the Gold Coast. It didn't work Mum. I got stuck. I just got stuck. I'm sorry. Is Dad ok? Can I—'
'Slow down. Where are you exactly? We'll get you home tonight.'
'Magic Mountain.'
'Honey, I'm not sure if I know where that is. Are you okay?'

'Fine. I just need to get home... Chairlift Ave, Nobby Beach, on the Gold Coast... in Queensland. This is exactly where I am... I'm on the street. I don't have anywhere to go. I want to leave now Mama?'

'Henry, get the credit card,' Joan Smith whispered to her eager husband.

The taxi interior glowed warm with sobering intimacy, fumes fell heavy and mean from the exhaust, and the driver, large in his seat, seemed all shoulders and neck from behind, like a bulldog stuffed in a tight shirt.

'The bus terminal, Surfers Paradise please. I think it's on Cavill Ave,' Ash said.

'Yeah luv, I know. It's all been fixed up don't worry,' he mumbled.

Her hands pressed together into her shallow lap. She had nothing left, except herself, and of that, she only felt half. The Gold Coast had stripped her bare, in every way, from every corner of herself. First, her body was a novelty, and she thought she wanted to be desired, then a prisoner, and she thought she wanted to be protected, and now a fugitive—she knew she needed to be free, and desired, and protected. Loved.

Ash felt childlike as she rode in the back seat, knowing she had somewhere to be and was grateful to be going to her dearly missed family home. Barefoot, in a bikini and sundress, her skin was a palette of bruises and bites, with tiny scars of small burrs with fine barbed awns, bindi eyes, on the pads of her weathered feet.

They burned with all the venom that had passed under-foot, as she ran from it all, leaving unrealised love in her wake. She was soothed as her soles rubbed on the freshly vacuumed floor mats. Her attention drifted to the blur of nights' pavements and pillars that blew past under the shadows of nothing. It was a long way, Nobby Beach to Surfers Paradise when circumstances weren't the best.

ↄ⌀

She touched every spotlit headrest, left then right, as she paced the narrow aisle of the Greyhound, finally choosing a window seat at the rear, on the left, so she could see the sunrise. Ash was sentimental like that, sometimes. The interior smelled like window cleaner, old vinyl and the lightest scent of patchouli, which she expected was from the middle-aged caftan wearing woman sitting a few rows behind the driver. The lady sat tall and elegant, with gold lion tamer hoops in her ears, looking like a gypsy with ancient pools for eyes, too large for her face and wickedly thick black hair. Ash settled into her seat, tucking her legs underneath like a foal. She considered the long ride home to Black Ridge, that stretched before her, giving time to unfold her thoughts.

Ash was well aware that she had allowed all of this to happen: love, hate, pleasure and pain. With enough hindsight falling at her feet, a collapsed house of cards, it was revealed in plain sight, in the back of the south-bound Greyhound—that the past ten months were punishment for living and not dying, dealt by her own hand. She didn't die, and she would never be able to repay Edie for that.

Healing lucidity had reigned upon Ash, as the bus merged onto the highway that carved through the grey evening scrub for a thousand miles more. Running from the promise of love may have been foolish, but if there was anything La Quinta had taught her, it was this: *You can't grow a flower in sand.* Her heart was broken, she broke it, and when it didn't hurt enough, she broke it more. Until she was sand, to her core. Her soul craved cathartic pain and suffering, punishment for living, and indeed, it had been delivered. Ash wasn't sure if she was done. Where would the hurt end? How much damage would it take? How much love would she have to ignore, and how much neglect would she have to endure? It was time to trust that the answers would present themselves. She had to trust Edie's wisdom that the universe always delivered.

Tora stood at the wide motel window, looking west onto the midnight street which had finally eased to the soft sway of the moon and lull of the restless tide. Nobody passed by. The burned ribs of Jay's caravan across the road lay invisible under the char black sky. Tora had expected to see Ash any moment, for every minute and hour that had passed since she slipped away. He was unable to wait any longer in that lover's room alone, sitting parched like those plastic flowers in the dry vase. Thirsty and hopeless. The day had seen him shift from one cell to another, with a constant yearning that never left him, not since that very first day. The first time he ever saw her face.

Tora left the motel and headed out onto the vacant streets to find Ash. At first he wasn't sure where to start. Then he realised he should simply start at the beginning.

Island Dreams was closing. The club was drained of most patrons, and the house lights were up, revealing a gaping, bruised room with tipped bar stools on a black concrete floor. A flock of mirror balls hovered over the sleepless glassie who was sweeping up smashed plastic from puddles of beer and cider in the mosh pit, grateful that glass had been outlawed the summer before, for obvious reasons.

Gina the Door Bitch was slumped at the bar, smoking a pink menthol cigarette, sipping vodka and soda lethargically through a too-long straw. Zoe was at her side, in a golden bikini with a blue beauty-pageant sash stained and twisted across her shoulder. She twirled her ponytail with her manicured fingers as she caught her own reflection beyond the crowd of spirits that stood shelved behind the bar.

When the girls saw Tora approach, they sat to attention, sucking in their washboard tummies. Gina tousled her perm and licked her lips. It had become an involuntary action on her part and had been going on for years.

'Tora Jones,' her hoarse voice purred. 'Hey baby. Just in time for a drink… with me… at my place, my husband won't mind,' Gina teased and then turned to face her drink. 'The bar's closed, sorry babes.'

'Ha. It's okay Geegee,' he kissed her cheek. 'I'm actually here to see Zoe.'

'Hey, Zoe. How ya doing? Big night in here by the look of it?'

'Yeah, the Miss Hawaiin Tropic heats started tonight,' Zoe blushed and unnecessarily pointed out the sash that crossed her glittered breasts.

'Right. You won? Cool… Hey, have you seen Ash around?'

'Ash? Jay's Ash? Nah, I haven't seen her since the night of the storm. She dropped by to visit right as it hit. So full on! She was acting weird and he came'n took her home. Poor thing he was worried sick about her… so relieved when he found her at my place—'

'Yeah… right. Thanks anyway.' Tora started to turn away.

'Hey Tora. If you're going back home, I've got something of Ash's here. Can you give it to her? She'd be missing it. Hang on. I'll just get it.'

Zoe slid her bronzed suntan-oil ass off the barstool and trotted into the darkness. She emerged with a fern green Tupperware box.

'Ash was clutching this for dear life at my place. Thanks for getting it to her.' Zoe handed Tora Ash's *firebox*.

Tora ambled back to Monaco Street, half-dazed and nauseous with hunger. He crossed the lawn and went into the estranged backyard with the slow and anticipated steps of a tumbleweed.

He balanced on the diving board nose, a tightrope threaded between his heart and hers. With stars in his hair, he stared down into the obsidian pool—a pale reflection of his silhouette, the only evidence of his existence, refracted and condensed, on an audience-less podium beneath the faded clouds. He looked low and deep into the black mirror for the longest time, waiting for an answer. He watched the west horizon stir to wakefulness as the sky grew pink with day and new light shone to reveal a glow of jellybean yellow, his skateboard left bogged in a puddle of broken teeth on a backdrop crestfallen colours. The scene reminded Tora of an abandoned carnival.

Ash's faded mural was rain-washed. Strands of detail still clung to the grit of the pool walls. Weeping pink trees peeked above a naive mountainous line of purple dust, underscoring something she had written in her own hand … *bla k ridg*. He jumped to his feet.

Ring. Ring. Ring. Ring–

    'Uh..huh.'
    'I need'ya car. I think she's gone home.'
    'What? I left it on 6th Ave. You know where the keys are.'

'Thanks man, I'll call you when I get there. Bye—'
'Hey Tora, I gotta go away a while.'
'Tokyo?'
'Well... not Black Ridge.'
'How'd you know? You're a fucking mystery dude.'
'Good luck. Go get her. Bye.'

The morning air hung, humid and still as a freshly sealed jam jar. Misty-eyed on the avenue, the Beast sat heavily with its nose pointed to the sea—a steed ready for pursuit into the unknown. On the bonnet, like a pirate's cat, Ninja scratched into the windscreen void hoping to snare a moth, a powdered brown and hysterical breakfast. Tora swept up the hungry cat and greeted her with a tickle behind the ear before putting her into the back seat along with his bag, skateboard and Ash's *firebox*. The horsepower roared to life, quick as a spark and Tora eased out of Palm Beach, ready for the open road.

CHAPTER TWENTY-ONE

Crimson & Clover

Jay's car windows were hazed with salted air when he was woken by crazed gulls. They swooped a nearby rubbish bin, scavenging old chips and berating each other with enraged fishwife cries. Greenmount headland, the gaping remains of a volcano, waded into the sea, bowed down in her emerald headdress as waves lurched at her rocky feet. The milky froth layered upon the surrounding sand and a cartel of blue bottles trimmed the shoreline, sapphire and cobalt blue, predatory, temporary. Nobody knew what the shore would deliver with each new day. Like a child presenting gifts to an inattentive Mother, passers-by stepped over remnants of the ocean's foley from the night past.

Jay wanted this sunrise to be his last. The last time he would see the horizon turn yellow to tangerine along its endless flat line. His feet crushed the tiny white seashells that littered the sand all the way to the shore.

The first rush of water cleansed his feet of clover and blood, remnants of the troubled night before. He fixed his leg rope and paddled out far into the early sea, long past the break. He paddled until he tired. He wanted to reach the sun.

The water seemed to level and breathe slowly once he passed a certain point. There were no more gulls, and the other surfers were small dark stains, intermittent in his view as he looked back to the shore that rose and fell under the sky. The esplanade store windows caught the fire of day and shone back hard to the sea.

Jay could hear the clap of water under the nose of his surfboard as he lay with his ear to the deck, eyes shut. He thought of loss. He thought it was all he knew. He knew that to love was to lose. It was inevitable. He knew that life's purpose was only to love. Only to lose.

He opened his eyes to the blind morning light that took hold of the ocean, tapping at each new unborn wave with its bright fingers. He decided not to forsake a broken ending, where sunshine eclipsed eternal darkness. He wanted a dark resolution. His ice-white surfboard was smeared red with his own sorry blood. He wanted it all out. He wanted to pour himself into the sea. Dissolve himself, sacrifice himself to *her, she, woman*— all of the women he'd lost to love. With a light-head, he meekly smiled before he soundlessly whispered one of her names, for the first time in what was maybe a thousand days. Then the sound came.

'Nina.'

Nebraska held the surfboard steady by the nose. Her drowned lips, a faded mauve rose. She rested her pearlescent chin and gazed at his closed face. His hair travelled his shoulders and pooled in his blood with crimson lustre.

'Jay,' she whispered to the sand of his brow. 'I am the sunshine.'

His sleeping eyes locked with hers.

'Save me,' he said.

CHAPTER TWENTY-TWO

Avalon

The Beast just flew, that's what all the boys said. If you wanted to get somewhere, fast, the Beast was the best car for the journey. Tora accelerated on the straight, 100—120—140kms an hour. The engine growled and murmured the sound of speed with a pulse that snapped the otherwise silent air along the narrow country highway.

Tora was excited, he had never been more sure about anything in his life. Today was the day. He found himself grinning at the thought of her, a slow dance unfolding in his heart. The way she twisted her hair on her index finger when she sat alone by the pool; and the way she would sip her tea in the early light—stolen moments, so delicate, as she tamed the steam of her cup into perfect weather. He'd marry that girl someday. He grinned wider and tuned the flailing radio signal once again. *Avalon*. Tora sang out of tune, wondering how he even knew the words. He felt free and happy like it was the very first time, lifted and in love. He would show her, words weren't enough, not anymore. A sign blurred across the passenger window. *Black Ridge 380km.*

In the rearview mirror, Tora saw the glint of Ash's mixed tape on top of the bag. The back seat was a far stretch. Ninja, also on the open bag, was half-buried in Tora's clothes, sound asleep in the sun. Lucky cat. Tora reached for the cassette tape, and after a few extended attempts, managed to retrieve it with the tips of his fingers while he kept the steering wheel aligned with the road, somewhat. He turned back to face the wheel, momentarily under control, until he saw a dark animal in his path—a roo. Tora touched on the brakes, nothing. He pressed again, and again harder, *nothing.*

༚

The Greyhound had rocked and lulled Ash to sleep somewhere after Ballina, but before Yamba. She was trying to stay awake for Yamba, she loved that place and had fond memories of being allowed to sleep on the beach, under the night sky, for the very first time as a child. Dreams weaved through her, detailed and intricate as a needlepoint, fixing her to the speeding stars above. The old oak tree by Edie's grave was leafless and uprooted like a burned claw clutching the cold air. In a howl of wind and torrent of rain, the earth was awash with indigo waves that pulsed with veins of crushed black ice; Ash was left naked on the ambling cemetery path unable to find Edie. The sound of Tora calling for

Ash, beyond the storm and the raging inland sea broke the dream, pulling her into the morning light.

Ash woke to see the sky glow warm and buttery as the light melted over the low mountains. Habitually, she put her hand to the window to touch the cool glass and the waved lines of the horizon. She studied her bare hand and tipped her head back, sombre. A sign, green and bright, leaned into view *Black Ridge 380kms*. Her heart skipped.

The bus broke its speed, slowed and finally stopped roadside, with a heave and sigh. Now in the middle of nowhere, the passengers looked to each other curiously as they waited for information or instructions. Ash looked down onto the glossy highway. There were skid marks and some papers and photos scattered with their corners lifting from the bitumen in the gentle morning breeze. Ash arced herself to see more and pressed her forehead hard against the glass only to see the full scale of the catastrophe. The papers on the road were her drawings. The smashed plastic was a cassette tape cover and the lime green in the distance, her *firebox*, gutted.

Ash felt her blood drain in the direction of the floor, a quivering pool of fear, low and dark beneath her. Hardly able to steady herself, she stood and shakily walked toward the front of the bus in slow motion. Through the bus windscreen, she could see the Beast, upside down and disjointed on the side of the road like one of those broken toys on La Quinta's front lawn. Ninja bounded around the wreckage and then into the scrub without care.

Ash stood on the quiet road, haunted. A crow cried in sympathy and then delight, and with that, Ash fell to her knees on the highway-side gravel. The bus driver came to Ash's aid, helping her to her feet. Time painfully slowed as she crossed the lanes toward the overturned car. Hardly touching the earth, she seemed to lose time with every step as reality slipped away. She peered into the black interior—it was empty.

Two men ran ahead, beyond the wreck into the baron landscape.

'Radio for an ambulance! There's a man. He's alive!' Someone yelled out to the bewildered driver.

Ash, hardly balanced on her own two feet, stumbled to the roadside clearing and found the men standing over Tora. He lay on his back motionless in the pale dirt. She crouched down to him, her hands on his face, gently searching for life.

'Don't leave me here. You can't go, not now,' she whispered. 'I'm with you. I won't run anymore. Please. Stay... please,' she sobbed.

Tora stirred slightly. He tried to open his eyes and take in a deeper breath. Through a squinted lens, he could see Ash's frame glowing in the sunlight, she appeared to hover in the breeze, and her eyes shone into his—in a way he'd never seen before. His mind-scape became ethereal as he floated between otherworldly realms. Hallucinations of love and death engulfed him.

With a fire in the head and fire in his heart, he let his imagination take hold, attuned to what his body was feeling—underwater, floating in the deep sea, with his one true love, embraced in golden wings of light, effortless, timeless he felt his body merge with hers. Then he heard himself speak.

'I'm gonna take you home. We're gonna be okay. I'm ok—'

Ash kissed his ear, light as a feather. 'I love you.'

She took hold of Tora's hand, strong and warm, her fingers entwined with his like the roots of that old oak tree. The mermaid ring on his pinkie winked, gilt with sun. He coughed painfully through broken ribs, and she touched his torso soft as a kitten. Ash settled beside him and decided to never let him go. Never ever.

When something of great value is put before you,
a treasure, take it when it is presented as yours.
Don't run. Don't hesitate. Don't wait. Be grateful and relish
the moment. Above all, be assured it could just as quickly be
taken away. So, grab it and hold on to it before you are left
with just another scar, open and never to heal.